AF434881

JALIYA

And the Secrets of the Golden Dragonfly

Michelle Masanza

JALIYA

Copyright @ Michelle Masanza, 2023 All rights reserved. No part of this publication may be reproduced, shared in any form or introduced into a retrieval system, or transmitted, by any means (electronic, mechanical, photocopying, recording, or otherwise) except for brief quotations in printed reviews, without prior written permission from the author.

ISBN: 978-9913-647-74-8
Edited by: Gawaya Tegule
Cover art by: Kofi Studios

To all the children to whom we entrust our future.

Contents

Acknowledgements

To my father Prof. Dr. Michael Masanza: Thank you for letting me draw on the furniture, cut up your sheets, and break down the walls of your house. You have given me the tools to create anything my heart desires and I owe everything I am to you.

To my mother, Hon. Dr. Monica Musenero Masanza: This story is as much yours as it is mine. Thank you for never letting me settle for less. Thank you for teaching me that success comes from doing those hard, annoying, boring, mundane tasks. Thank you for always giving me a platform to learn, grow, and freely express myself. You have always been my number one fan and supported every crazy idea, never once dismissing me. More than anything, thank you for being my friend.

To my brothers, Joshua and Joel who have supported me at every step of my journey: Thank you for the endless hours spent laughing and dreaming and creating together. Thank you for the hugs and words of encouragement. And thank you for always challenging me to think bigger and be better.

To myself: When you read this in the years to come, I hope it will be a constant reminder of your strength. I hope it reminds you that you are unstoppable and can achieve anything you put your mind to. I hope it inspires you to dream and bring about a better future for your generation. The best is yet to come!

PART ONE

"The child who is not embraced by the village will burn it down to feel its warmth"

-African Proverb-

***

Shattered Mirage

"Why do I have to suffer for their choices?!"

After bearing the burden of their secrets for the past six months, I wasn't any closer to an answer. I was tired of waiting around as my life slowly crumbled around me. Finally, I had reached my breaking point. The decision to run away wasn't an easy one.

I loved my family. Despite my father's control, and his distant approach to raising me, or my mother's inability to stand up to him as he treated her like an ornament, they were still my family.

I grew up in a comfortable four-bedroom home in the suburbs around Kampala. If you had visited at some point during my childhood, you would have been greeted with a well-manicured lawn in front of a house hedged on all sides with emerald green bushes and ornate flower beds.

The smell of a freshly cooked meal would have flooded your senses in the afternoon and my parents might have entertained you over tea and home-backed scones in the yard until the meal was ready. I will always look back on those days fondly.

Though my family was dysfunctional, I was always grateful to have both my parents in my life.

My mother was initially a stay-home mom but started her own business when I was around thirteen, which was when I was deemed competent enough to not need her constant supervision. It seemed like from the day I was born she watched my every move. If I was caught doing anything remotely suspicious, a swift hand would fall onto my shoulder, reminding me to behave. Being the only child of a middle-class Ugandan family during the 90s was my only true crime.

And what was the punishment for this crime? A painful lack of social skills led me to have almost no friends for most of my childhood. I loved to read and draw and spent most of my after-school evenings in my father's massive study/office reading through his collection of books. It's not like I had anything more childlike to do. From law, economics, finance, personal growth, and business development, I had managed to get through about fifty-five percent of his massive collection by the time I was twelve. From time to time I would sneak one of the novels I wasn't allowed to read into my room, finish it all night and then return it the next morning before school like nothing ever happened. This was the most exciting part of my days until one night when I was thirteen when my mother found one of the novels I had stashed away under my pillow, ready for an exciting night of reading. I got into way more trouble than I thought I could possibly get into and I was banned from going into the library for a year! I had to tell my mother what book I wanted to read and have her fetch it for me. How ridiculous.

The scenic days of my childhood ended at that point and I began to notice just how strange my life was. Up until that point, the control my parents had over my life was masked by the glistening images of happy afternoons in the yard with my parents as I impressed their guests with my reading and writing skills. They seemed to be so proud of me back then.

When that veil was lifted, I realized that in every aspect of my life whether it was school, friendships, and even what I wore, my parents had the final say and my opinion was more of a formality. The decisions were made by them behind closed doors and I was never privy to those conversations.

If I was ever upset or discontented with a decision they had made, my mom would try to calm me down by saying, *"It's okay Jaliya. Your father and I are only doing what we know is best for you."*

Convincing my mother to advocate for me behind those closed doors was the only way I could have a say in anything. But sometimes she wasn't around and I had to deal with whatever new law my father laid down. She didn't leave very often but when she did, she would take mysterious trips for months on end at seemingly random intervals to God knows where.

Once, when I was around six or seven years old, I wanted so desperately to go on the school's annual trip to the zoo with my class. Six years had been plenty of time to study my parents and I knew that a school field trip was not something that they would have agreed to. *"That's a whole day you could spend practicing your French,"* I imagined my father would say. Well, learning French wasn't what I felt like I wanted to spend that day doing! This was Uganda anyway. What good was French here?

That was the first time I remember hatching a detailed plan to get my way. I began weeks before the trip with the occasional comment about how cool animals are and how much I loved them. I collected all the books in my father's library about animals, birds, and fish and only read those for two weeks. A key part of my plan was making sure I was on my best possible behavior. Eventually, I started steering every conversation to the topic of the zoo and how I would love to go. When the school finally announced the annual trip, I begged and pleaded with my mother to let me go. To her credit, she did hold out for two weeks but eventually relented and promised to talk to my father about it.

That day I stood outside my father's study door waiting eagerly for my mother to come out and tell me if I would get to go. In the end.... I did not get to go to the zoo with all the other six-year old's in my class. But I did learn a valuable lesson. I could never cheat the system.

Boarding school was the first time I was away from both my parents, but more importantly, it was the first time I was away from their omnipotent control and ever-watchful eyes. Something changed in me during my first

year in boarding school as I began to realize just how different I was from the other students around me.

All the girls in my dorm seemed to care much more about gossip and vanity than they did about their studies! I had noticed this in primary school, but my parents always said that secondary school was a much different ballgame that I had to take seriously.

That statement might have been true to some extent, but something about how un-burdened my schoolmates seemed to be made me question my all- knowing parents. They didn't seem to be as anxious as I did and didn't care for the perfectionist tendencies my parents had instilled in me.

Year after year I began to care less and less about scores and grew more interested in having fun and exploring who I was. I read whatever books I wanted, made new friends, and spoke to women other than my mother about the issues every growing girl faced. I discovered my passion for creative arts and learned so much about who I was. I realized that there were a lot of really bad things in this world that I wanted to do something about. My world grew bigger and brighter before my eyes, and slowly, the sunny front yard that had been the center of my universe began to shrink.

I spent the holidays between terms at my friends' houses talking for hours on end about everything and nothing. How did I get my helicopter parents to let me go? Well, the school had encouraged parents to let their children study in groups throughout the holidays and what parent could argue against that? My parents, of course, grew tenser as the years went by, and constantly complained that I had changed because of the kids I was hanging out with.

Though I grew bolder and began to argue with them a lot more, I always kept my grades up and respected the rules that they set, coming back home on time and introducing all my friends to them. I didn't want to give them any reason to take back whatever freedoms I had acquired.

I loved every minute of my secondary school years. I learned to love and appreciate the colours in the sky and always noticed the breeze rustling through the trees as I and my friends walked from our dorm rooms to class. They always complained that my mind was elsewhere and they weren't wrong. I felt like I had to make up for lost time. I finally had reference points to put my life against and put a finger on what had always seemed off about my life. I could finally see the contrast and make decisions for myself. I was growing.

When I came home from school after sitting my Form Six exams, I found myself in a strangely silent and melancholic state. I knew that the freedom I had found away from home was gone. University would have been the natural next step but I wanted to do something else before I dove right back into academia. A lot was weighing on my mind and I had no one to talk to. I was growing tired of my father's nagging about how I was wasting time. What I needed was time. Time to decide what I wanted to do with my life before I spent more of it chasing after a piece of paper.

Forthefirstmonthathome,Iwould
tell my father something along the lines of, "Dad, please give me some time, I just got home

from school and the exam period drained me." This was never satisfactory, but it would silence him until a few days later when he would bring it up again. My mother grew concerned but stayed silent on the matter.

After six months of this back and forth, the tension in the house was so thick, you could cut through it with a panga (machete)!

One night I and my mother were chatting away as I helped her make dinner. The kitchen was a fairly big room, with tall walls and two large windows that went all the way up to the ceiling. I stood at the counter staring out of the massive window as I had so often done.

Though it wasn't required of me because we always had a maid, I liked to help my mom out in the kitchen since she didn't let the maid cook for my father. That was a task this African woman would never delegate.

I stood over the counter, chopping up some green pepper (bell peppers) for my mom, and we talked about life. She was telling me a story from her childhood that she had told me about a hundred times and I was laughing along with her, finishing her sentences, as I had all but memorized the story at that point. I handed her the chopping board with all the finely chopped ingredients, proud of myself for the professional job I had done, and went back to my spot at the counter.

I could see the night sky out of the big window in front of me and couldn't help but get lost in it. I noticed the inky blue background upon which the shimmering stars danced and I felt like walking up there and dancing with them. I watched wispy clouds cover up the crescent moon from time to time and closed my eyes as I listened to the cool, steady breeze rustle through the leaves of the old mango tree outside the kitchen.

My mom looked back at me and gently smiled as she had gotten used to how her daughter's mind liked to wander off to some more peaceful corner of the world.

"Mom,"

I spoke feeling her gaze on my back as I kept staring off into the distance.

"what's the matter?"

She walked up to me, gently tapped my shoulder,

"Are you back from your trip to the moon?"

I snapped out of my trance with a jolt as I hadn't noticed how close she was and chuckled at her witty comment. I replied, "Unfortunately I am."

She tilted her head as she turned me towards her. *"Jaliya, I can't lie and say that I am not worried about you."*

Her slight smile turned to concern and her brow furrowed as she continued,

"I know your father puts a lot of pressure on you. But you are his only child. You know he wants the best for you. You've grown into a determined and headstrong young woman and have been nothing but a blessing to me. You know I'm proud of you"

With a sigh, she moved her palm from my shoulder and continued,

"But you've been at home for almost six months, and we are worried that you've grown so cold. You are no longer interested in school and don't seem to get out of your room unless it's to help me with the chores. We didn't like it when you spent so much time hanging out with your friends; getting into God knows what trouble, but this worries us even more."

As I watched her struggle to find the words to say what she wanted to say, a bitter coppery taste crept into my mouth.

"Mom, I think what your trying to say is, 'Jaliya, why aren't you talking about university?' right?" I said, mimicking her slow but elegant way of speaking.

She looked a little put off by how bluntly I had said it. The words certainly did not fit the tone. But I could see that I had hit the nail on the head.

I grabbed a rag and began to wipe down the counter as I continued,

" I'm not the little girl you couldn't let out of your sight for even a moment. Me taking some

time for myself at arguably one of the most defining times of my life isn't that strange. I know that university is important, but I just don't feel like I am ready to take that on. I just want to take some time to live my life and get to know myself a little better. Is that so strange?"

Saying it out loud for the first time, even I could tell how lame that excuse sounded.

"Jaly," my mother said in an uncharacteristically stern voice, *"You can discover who you are anywhere. Even as you study."*

I flinched. She wasn't buying it. Unlike my father who would have dropped it by now, mother wasn't as easily placated and she was certainly not amused.

The truth, at least part of it was that I was resentful of how my life had always been boiled down to my studies and how well I behaved. Everything always came back to that. I had long begun to despise how much of my worth was determined by that paper and how much society seemed to desperately need it from me. Especially when there were more pressing matters at hand. But these were things I couldn't explain to her at the moment.

She could tell that I was holding something back and continued more sympathetic this time.

"Jaly, you and I both know your father won't stand this much longer. Okay, maybe we can convince him to let you take a gap year before you go to medical school, but..."
A chill went down my spine and I froze. As she kept speaking my thoughts drowned out her voice.
"Medical school! When did they make that decision? What about me screams doctor?!" I was pissed but now was not the time for an outburst. I had to stick to the plan. I spoke out loud but slower, actively trying to filter the next words that came out of my mouth.
"I don't think I have ever told you that I wanted to go to medical school, and by the way you said it, it seems that I don't have many options. You always do this, Mom. You and Dad make decisions about my life without so much as asking what I want and I am always expected to just go with it. For how long?"

"We only do that because we know what's best for you," she said, back to that stern and cold tone.

"And how is that what's best for me?" I asked, *"All it has done in the past is make me miserable! It's like I am living life for the both of you."*

"Jaliya! Don't speak to your mother like that!" my father's voice boomed from behind me. The man always appeared out of nowhere at the worst times, like a ghost in the night, scaring me

halfway to my grave. Admittedly my attempt to hold back my emotions had failed. I had wanted to talk to my mother alone but now that he was here, I knew that if I was going to get anywhere, I couldn't back down.

He stood under the arched entrance of the kitchen, and my mom immediately walked up to him, trying to calm him down. His six-foot-seven frame dwarfed her as he gently pushed her to the side. He walked up to me and crossed his arms as I craned my neck to look up into his eyes. Glaring at me in disapproval was a tactic he often used on me as a child, and when he did, I would look down at the ground, pale with fear, ashamed for whatever I had supposedly done. This time I refused to turn away. I looked straight into his eyes and returned his glare with the same intensity. He did not like this and his expression grew fiercer.

His deep, steady voice boomed off the walls of the kitchen and it took every ounce of courage in my bones not to break my gaze.

"I have put up with your nonsense for long enough. Your results came out months ago, and I refuse to coddle you any longer. I have made an appointment for us to meet the dean of the school of medicine at one of the top universities in Kampala, and your place is all but granted."

I shook as it dawned on me once more just how little control I had over the situation. It would have been easier for everyone in that room if I had just done what he said. Unfortunately, for both me and my parents, this time I couldn't afford to back down.

"How are you getting out of this one Jaliya?" I thought to myself as I began to panic. I looked over my options and found that I had only two; Negotiation and Rebellion.

"Dad, I don't want to be a doctor," I said timidly at first.

"What was that!!!?" he boomed at me.

I closed my eyes, swallowed my fear, and opened them again to meet his right where I had left them. I repeated myself emphasizing every word.

"I-don't-and-have-never-wanted-to-be-a-doctor. I don't know where you got that idea from because I don't remember you ever asking me about it."

I had done it now. I didn't know what happens next since I had never stood my ground for this long. My mind raced with horrible predictions of my fate but even then, I kept my gaze.

He let out a heavy sigh as he brought his right hand up to his brow. *"We want you to have a stable life in a respectable field. What is wrong with becoming a doctor?"* he finally pleaded.

I didn't expect him to try negotiation and was caught off guard by the sincerity in his voice.

"Seems I do get to try negotiation," I thought to myself. Deciding whether or not I could trust his change in demeanor. I made my case.

"There is nothing wrong with being a doctor. I just know that I would be miserable. Don't you both want me to live a life in which I am fulfilled and happy...."

My mother cut me off,

"Jaliya, that's not how life works. You've had plenty of time to run around with those ideas in your head, but they need to remain in those useless novels you read."

I could feel my chest tighten as she continued. The one thing that had always brought me and my mother together was our shared love for books and the blissful escape they gave us both.

Back when she had caught me with the novel and my father punished me harshly for it, she apologized when I came back from school and gave the book back to me. She explained that we had to follow Father's rules so I had to keep this between me and her. She would tell me how she too used to spend hours reading and how I reminded her of her younger self, which encouraged me to read more and more. From then on we had shared a bond to the joy

that those novels she smuggled. But now here she was, calling them *"useless"*. She had hit me where it hurt. It didn't hurt because I was angry at her. It hurt because I knew why she had to say that. I felt nothing but sadness for both her and my father. I knew that forcing me to do anything wasn't what they wanted
but something they had to do to keep me safe.

But I also couldn't accept my fate as the family's sacrificial lamb. My life was my own, and I was going to do everything to make that known.

As these thoughts went through my head, my heart ached and tears filled my eyes. *"I need to be alone for now,"* I said, throwing the rag on the counter and rushing past my father. My mother tried to come after me, but he stopped her.

I locked the door to my room and threw myself on my bed. Soon the stream of tears had turned into a raging river as I wept into my pillow. I was feeling a lot of conflicting emotions. As much as I wanted to stay there curled up in a ball, I had to stop them. I calmed myself saying, Jaliya, get a grip. The time for these tears has passed and will come again. *"You need to remember why you are doing this"*

It was too late to turn back now. I had already decided that I was going to save myself and my parents from a puppet's fate. I was the

one who had to protect them now. Would I be
strong enough to do it?

A Hiding Place

Did I have a plan? No. I had no idea what to do next. I could never answer the *"What do you want to be when you grow up?"* question all the aunties loved to ask. And now I found myself at a literal crossroads with no inkling of a plan.

What were we arguing about this time? I can't even remember. All I know is that I was sick of him acting like my life was his second chance to live his unrealized dreams. And that's how I found myself outside our black gate with the small suitcase I had crammed a few of my belongings into. I had taken that suitcase with me every time I had gone to school but this time, I wasn't planning to come back. I was officially homeless.

As I stood staring at the dusty road on that hot Kampala day, I could feel my heart pounding in my throat. I was sweating from the storm of packing I had just completed and needed to catch my breath. The five hundred thousand (Ugandan shillings) tucked away in the small leather purse haphazardly slung over my shoulder was the only money I had to my name.

That morning, I had set my plan into motion at the breakfast table.

"Good morning, Father," I said, taking my seat at the opposite end of the table. I was afraid that if I sat any closer, he would smell my fear.

"Good morning," he replied without setting down the newspaper he was reading.

"Where is Mom?" I asked, noticing that my mother wasn't at her place next to my father.

"She went on one of her work trips. She will be back the day after tomorrow," he replied still holding the newspaper up.

I was saddened by this. I would have loved to see her one last time, but there was no time for such sentiments. For the time being, I was content to sit in silence eating my breakfast, a cup of warm spiced African tea with two slices of bread slathered in a margarine spread.

Once I was done, it was time for phase two of the plan. I took a deep breath, dug up all the courage within me and as I stood up to clear the table, I finally spoke.

"Uhm. Father, I'm sorry for the way that I acted last night. I just really need more time to figure some things out before I go to university."

He threw the newspaper down and glared at me, back to his combative way of doing things.

"I don't want to hear any of this anymore. I made it very clear last night that the decision has already been made. There is a student exchange program with the U.S. in the second year of the medical course so you can get away from us if that is what you really want." He took a loud sip from his cup of tea and looked up at me as if to say, *"You can't argue against this."*

This was the second time he had tried to "negotiate" and whilst it was an admirable attempt to extend an olive branch, I had already chosen violence. As for how in the world he jumped from Uganda to the opposite side of the world I didn't know. Something must have happened that night that I wasn't aware of. In any case, his decorum made the tantrum I was about to throw a little less justifiable. He had no idea what a performance I was about to put on.

I slammed the tray of cups onto the table just hard enough for them to make a terrible noise. *"WHAT??? IN THE U.S. I've never been more than an hour away from you and Mom. How can you think of sending me to the U.S.? We have no family or friends there!"*

I could see the rage build in his eyes as he watched the cups almost fall and break. If there was one thing my father hated, it was an unnecessary racket.

"What is wrong with you Jaliya? When did you start thinking talking back to your father was acceptable?"

And now for phase three, I had to turn on the waterworks. Tears began to blur my vision and my hands fell to my side in seeming defeat.

"What is unacceptable is how you think you can puppeteer my life! I've done everything you have ever told me to do. Have I not earned the right to make some of my own choices?" Father hated it when I cried. Not that he felt bad about making me so sad, it's quite the opposite. It was a sign of weakness and he found it distasteful.

"Can you stop crying and act like an adult for once? If you don't want to go abroad that's fine. But let me make one thing clear to you. This is my house. And as long as you're in my house, you will do as I say. If you don't like that, then you are welcome to leave."

He leaned back into his chair and went back to reading his paper.

"But father...," I tried to say, the trickle of tears now a full downpour.

"Can you get out of here now? I've had enough of your nonsense," he barked.

I flinched and booked it to my room slamming the door behind me for dramatic effect. *"That was a lot easier than I thought,"* I said to myself wiping away my crocodile tears. Even I was almost convinced by my performance.

Phase four was pretty straightforward, pack a bag and leave before anyone notices. Now that he had technically kicked me out, my disappearance wouldn't raise too many questions. All I needed was for him to utter those words, after all, he did make himself very clear. I knew they would eventually start looking for me, but his pride would buy me some time.

I don't know how long I stood in front of that black gate, but it was about 7 p.m. when I picked up the little brown suitcase and walked down that marram road toward my new life.

I decided that the most sensible thing to do at that moment was to go to Maria. Maria had been my best friend for years and knew me better than I knew myself. She had recently moved into a hostel near the university she was attending and was honestly the only option I had.

I waved down a boda (motorcycle taxi) on the main road a few turns away from my house and boarded to the university town, which cost about seven thousand shillings from where we lived in the suburbs. There was no way I was paying that ridiculous amount. After a lengthy back and forth with the boda guy, he finally brought it down to five thousand shillings. Still high, but it was late and I was tired, so I strapped my bag to the back of the bike and we rode off into the sunset.

As the wind blew past my face, I felt peace fill my soul for the first time in months. It was as if all the anxiety of living under constant lock and key was finally melting away. The knot that had formed in my throat during the fight with my father loosened and I felt the tears flow.

"Why am I crying?" I thought to myself, *"I'm finally free. I get to live my own life now, so why am I sad?"*

Looking back now, I think it was my heart breaking. Despite all the anger in my heart, I still loved my father and mother and felt bad for playing such a cruel game. In the coming years, I would realize just how big of a mistake this move was.

Maybe if I had realized that, I would have turned back and made amends with my father. Maybe I could have skipped the hell I was about to go through. Maybe I would have put aside my ego and realized that there was a shard of wisdom in the shattered pane that was my father's way of *"love"*.

It took about fifteen minutes to get to my destination. I paid my fare, carried my luggage, and waddled my way through dimly lit alleys, corridors, and stairwells to get to

Maria's one-bedroom, single- person hostel that was part of a fairly large complex.

It was about 7:30 p.m. and the sun was on its way out but not completely gone. I finally got to the fairly well-lit courtyard walled on all sides by storied hostel blocks. I made my way up the stairs to the second floor of the block I knew Maria was staying at. I had been there once before and was trying my best to remember which of the twelve rooms on the floor was hers.

Somehow by the grace of Heaven, I knew which one was hers the moment I walked by and knocked on her door. I hadn't seen her for a couple of weeks, and the last time we spoke on the phone I was lamenting my plight, so I didn't know how she would react to seeing me.

When Maria opened the door, she gave me a strange look and let out what I can only describe as a crackle. *"HEE HEEEEE! So, you finally ran away from home your girl?!"*
I replied as I took off my boots, and run to

throw myself on her queen-sized bed.
I knew she was half joking so I laughed along with her as I took off my boots and ran to her queen-sized bed.
"It was bound to happen sooner or later. Today just happened to be the day."

Her room was small but quite cozy. It was about 13 × 10m, with one big window on the wall across from the door. Her white lace curtains brought so much elegance to the space that had very little in the way of furniture.

The room consisted of her fairly large bed against the wall with a window, a desk on the right wall, and a wardrobe on the left wall. She had potted plants on nearly every horizontal surface and one, in particular, sat on top of the wardrobe and had its vines trail down the side facing the window.

Maria's room was as calm and serene as she was. She was an organized and well-managed person who always had a plan and seemed to have all her goats in a row. I couldn't help but wonder how we had stayed friends for so long.

As I lay drowning in the many pillows on her bed, Maria pulled me from my trance. *"Hey, Jaliya! You haven't answered me. Have you left home for good? That suitcase seems to confirm this, but I want to hear it from you,"* I had thought she was joking but apparently not. Regardless I didn't want to talk about what just happened and needed to divert the conversation.

"Is that how you welcome a guest? How un- African of you," I joked.

She giggled at my witty comment. You see, Maria was mixed race. Her father was Scottish but her mother, who raised her, was Ugandan. She always joked about how she would never depart from the way of the African that her mother had taught her. I thought she would at least get a little defensive and the topic would change but she continued to stare at me, waiting for me to answer her question. The *"not this time"* look on her face echoed her resolve. Guess we were going to talk about it.

"Ria, I can't live under the same roof as that man anymore. I think I'll spontaneously combust if I have to hear one more lecture from him."

She shot me a disappointed glance and crossed her arms.

"I'm guessing you haven't told your mom."

I buried my face back into the pillows hoping they would hide me forever as the conversation with my mother the night before replayed in my mind. *"She's part of the problem!"*

Maria laughed as she carried my suitcase and boots from the door where I had left them and placed them down next to her wardrobe.

"Jaliya, you know you're welcome anytime, but as your friend, I have to tell you that you need to think these things through a little better. I know you have your differences with your father, and you and your mother aren't on the best terms, but we have to figure something out. From how pensive you looked a

few minutes ago, I'm not going to push it too much tonight. But tomorrow we are going to have a serious talk about your......situation."

If only she knew just how much thought, I had put into this decision.

I wanted to defend myself, but I took her up on her offer to not think about it anymore. She had always been like a second mother to me and always knew what to do when I found myself in these.... situations.

That night we had rolex (an omelet wrapped in a chapatti) and talked till one o'clock in the morning. I don't remember much about that conversation, but I know I vented about my father and the sorry state of my life without giving too much away.

After listening to me all night, Maria fell asleep. I on the other hand lay awake for hours. It was then, in the silence and darkness of my best friend's room that the anxiety I had earlier forgotten came flooding back.

I was no longer in my father's clutches for the time being, but there were much bigger demons chasing me, and I couldn't run away from them forever. I could no longer use his controlling nature as a crutch and had to take full responsibility for the part I had to play in the storm that I was about to be thrust into. Of course, these are the reflections of a much older and much wiser Jaliya that can put words to the emotions I was feeling. But at that moment, all I could feel was the weight of my family's future on my shoulders.

The next morning, Maria was up before the sun. My early rising habits had died off nine months ago when I closed the high school chapter of my life and I was highly offended when her stirring woke me up since it was a Saturday, the most righteous of days! Did she have no heart?! But, then, I quickly remembered that I was the homeless one in this situation and with humility, I bit my tongue.

As the morning went on, I freshened up in the communal bathroom at the end of the hallway which reminded me again of high school when I wanted so much to forget it.

We had our black tea and chapatti breakfast and sat down for our scheduled chat.

It was about 8 a.m. and the crisp golden sunlight flooded the room. The light danced across the green and sage-variegated leaves of the vines growing from atop the wardrobe as the gentle breeze flowed in. I couldn't help but notice how different this was from the drama of the mornings at home. They usually consisted of trying to avoid starting a fight with my father until I eventually triggered him. Then I would have to listen to him lecture me about everything I am doing wrong and how I should fix it.

I watched my friend sit down on the floor

across from me with a pen and spiral notepad in her hand and couldn't help but wonder once more how it was that we were so different. In the four hours we were awake, she had swept and mopped her room, done all the dishes from last night, washed her clothes for the week, taken a shower, done her hair, put on a decent outfit, and probably solved world hunger!

And there I was, hair looking like a marabou stork's nest on top of my head, wearing the same shirt she had given me to sleep in (now covered in food and toothpaste stains), and my mind plotting the quickest path back under the sheets.

I would often joke that I could turn my life around with only 2% of her power. And that's exactly what she was planning to do as she scribbled down a few headings on different pages of the notepad and color-coded them with the pack of highlighters that I was convinced were an extension of her body.

She held one of the highlighters in the air and a beaming smile covered her face as she handed it to me.

"Okay Jaliya, are you ready to
get your life together?"

I couldn't help but chuckle at how cartoonish she looked after being so serious just a second ago.

*"You make it sound like it's so easy.
I've been trying to 'get my life together' for the
past nine months."*

She laughed and placed the highlighter in
my hand with vigor. And spelled it out for me.
*"Well my dear, you don't have a choice. You are
homeless Jaliya. H-O-M-E-L-E-S-S,"*

It stung when I said it to myself but
hearing it from someone else was on another
level.

"Nawe, you don't have to say it like that."

*"I don't think you understand what I'm
saying Jaliya. I didn't want to tell you this last
night because you had just been kicked out..."*

"Kicked out?" I interrupted, *"I was not
kicked out. I chose to leave."*

"Whatever it was, you are here now,"
she said with a heavy breath.

*"Listen, I'm leaving this place and
moving in with my aunt who lives nearby so I
can save the money I've been paying....."*
"What!" I exclaimed.

My heart sank to the bottom of my feet,
and a cold chill went down my spine.

*"Jaliya calm down. It's not like I'm
throwing you out on the street."* I jumped to my
feet. *"You might as well be,"*

*"I'm still here for six months, so...we
have six months to get you on your feet,"* she
said.

I don't know whether it was bad luck or if the heavens were against me, but for the past nine months, I was not only trying to get my life together, but to save it!

"Jaliya, I know you don't want to go to University because you felt your dad was pushing you, but we could at least find a certificate or a diploma, something you can do so you can do in the meantime."

Her words stabbed me in my gut. I had hidden it so well up until this point, even going as far as running away to try and keep things from dissolving under my feet. But the moment I felt I was taking a step forward, something pulled me four steps back! If only I could explain to her that University wasn't the problem, or that my father wasn't the problem. But I couldn't. what excuse would I give this time? Would I run away from her too when she gets sick of me leaching off her?

I couldn't hide it anymore. The secrets I was keeping had begun to eat through my relationships. How long before they killed me?!

As badly as I wanted to tell her all of this, I couldn't. These were not her problems and dragging her into them was the last thing I wanted to do. It was a mistake to go to her for help. What help could she give? I couldn't even tell her the truth. I looked at the ground in defeat.

"I can't do that,"

"What do you mean you can't do that? It's not like I'm going to force you to do something you hate Jaliya. Pick a course you like and do that."

As she continued I could hear the frustration rising in her voice. *"I know you hate being 'forced' to do anything, but you have to be realistic. You don't know where your mom is, and you've burned the bridge with your dad. You refuse to get a job and have also tossed the idea of going to university into the trash. I'm trying to help you, but I can't be there to bail you out for the rest of your life. You need to stand on your own two feet before you become a burden."*

The moment that the last word slipped out of her mouth her hand came flying to try and stop it but it was too late.

"Jaliya, you know I didn't mean it like that," she said trying to soothe the situation.

Her words hurt because they were true. I fell back onto the bed and tears began to stream down my face. She was right. I had been living my life like a game of roulette but now things were too real for me to handle. I couldn't hide for the rest of my life.

Welcome To My Enemy

"Jaliya," Maria called softly after letting me cry for a few minutes. *"This isn't just about university, is it? You need to tell me what's going on."*

I slowly turned my face to her and whatever resolve I previously had completely failed me.

"I...I messed up, Maria. All I wanted was.... was to...to...to know the truth. I.... I got into some stupid.... club of kids and listened to that crazy man. But then they are watching his every move and I .... Put everyone's life on the line. It's only a matter of time before they find him again and then it's all over."

Chocking on every word I spoke, my heart pounded as the room began to spin around me. Up until this point I had kept everything buried away but as I said it out loud for the first time, the reality of my situation finally set in and I began to panic. I tried to pull back the tide of fear but it was too late. I was nearly suffocating under the weight of the words clawing their way out of me all at once.

Maria looked at me, horrified by what she was hearing. She got up and rushed to get me some water to drink from the jug on her table and tried to calm me down.

"Jaliya, please slow down. I don't understand what you're trying to say. Please take some water and calm down"

I couldn't hear her. My thoughts flashed back to the images of him, franticly scrambling through his pile of papers. All I could see were his desperate eyes as he pleaded for me to help him. My vision blurred and my feet began to go numb. I began to stumble for the door, muttering to myself as Maria's voice faded into a distorted whisper. I had to get out of that room.

"What have I done? What on earth have I done? I shouldn't have come here. Of course, they will find me. Why did I think I could hide?. I need to go find
him...."

As my hand reached through the haze for the door. I heard it......
KNOCK!KNOCK!KNOCK!
Three loud crashes came blaring from the door. The heart that had been beating so fast in my chest immediately sank to my feet. The blood drained from my limbs and I ran to the opposite end of the door.

"They've found me! They've found me!

They've found me!"

I whispered these words to myself as I desperately scanned the room for an escape. As I shuffled onto the bed towards the window, Maria pulled me back and viciously shook me.

"JALIYA! Have you gone mad? Get away from the window." Staring back at her I wondered if this was what insanity was. It didn't matter what she said, I needed to get out of there as soon as possible.

KNOCK!KNOCK!KNOCK!

This time louder. Maria sat me down on the bed and walked towards the door.

"Who in the world is trying to knock down my door."

I reached out to stop her and begged her not to open it, sobbing even more than I had before.

"Please....please don't open that door."

She clasped my hand and assured me it was probably just her landlord or another friend but that did nothing to calm me down.

"Who is it?" she called out and waited for a response. Seconds passed and none came. She called out again but still no reply.

"Calm down, okay. I'll just go take a look and be right back."

As Maria got closer to the door, the ringing in my ears grew louder and louder till it was defining. Time seemed to slow down as the lace curtains framing the window behind me fluttered lazily in the wind, almost frozen in place.

I don't know what it was, maybe intuition or maybe whatever God looking down on me had decided to give me a glimpse of what was to come. All I could feel at that moment was impending doom. When Maria opened the door, a familiar voice came from the other side.

"Is Jaliya here?" It was my mother. I let go of the breath I was holding and a wave of relief rushed over me. As Maria ushered her in she looked at me with concern and confusion.

"Jaliya…. It's your mother. Please come in, Mama Jaliya."

My mother stepped into the room and although the voice I had heard seconds prior was hers, I almost couldn't recognize her.

In the 20 years she had been married to my father, she always wore some frumpy, obnoxiously floral, shapeless gowns that looked more like maternity dresses than anything else. Her hair was always under a scarf or bonnet and even when it was *"done"*, it was in a plain up-do style. You could never tell looking at how she dressed that my mother was nearly 15 years younger than my father!

It had been less than 48 hours since I had seen her last but she looked like a completely different person.

Her hair was pulled back into a sleek bun and she wore a long-sleeved black buttoned-down shirt neatly tucked into a knee-length pencil skirt just as black as the shirt. Draped over her shoulders, a jet- black, knee-length blazer with a gorgeous golden dragonfly broach pinned onto the lapel. My focus was drawn to the little broach as it reflected the sunlight. It was nothing but bad news. Every time I saw that broach, sorrow was soon to follow. As she walked towards me all I could think was how menacing and frightful she looked in her all- black outfit. I was glad to see that the mask she had worn for so many years was finally off.

I stared at her, taking in this unfamiliar sight. Of all the terrible things that I had imagined were waiting for me behind that door, she was the one I was most relieved to see. Though I was glad it wasn't worse, this was still very bad and a debate raged inside my head. On the one hand, all I wanted was to jump into my mother's arms for comfort as I had done so many times as a child. But on the other hand, I knew why she was here and how she had found me so fast. If she knew where I was, so did they.

Mother gently placed a hand on my shoulder and, with the grace and elegance she always carried herself with, knelt on the floor in front of me. At least that's one thing that hadn't changed.

"Jaliya, my girl, what on earth were you thinking? Do you have any idea how worried I was when your father called me last night?"

The concern in her eyes as she spoke looked genuine, but my suspicion only grew. If my trust was what she wanted, she had made a mistake showing up dressed like one of them.

"Get your hands off me," I whispered, coldly brushing her hands off my shoulders and walking to the other side of the room. Disgust had taken the place of apathy on my face as I turned my back to her.

She calmly rose, gently dusted her knees, and turned to look my way.

Maria must have been shocked by what she was seeing. She was so used to the warm relationship between me and my mother, and she couldn't wrap her head around this frigid display.

"Jaliya, you can't talk to your mother like that. She came all this way and was probably worried sick about you."

"It's okay, Maria. My daughter has had a traumatic few months. Don't be too hard on her. I'll take her back home and we'll have a chance to talk all this over."

And then she addressed me.

"But your friend is right, Jaliya. I raised you to respect the hand that feeds you." The way she phrased that statement. Did she know how gross and distasteful it sounded?

*"If you get to choose at will when and when not to be my mother, then I get to choose when I'm sick of being your daughter, **Talika**!"*

Both Maria and my mother gasped in shock at my words. Maria because she had never heard me refer to my mother by her first name, and my mother because she hadn't heard that name in years.

I turned and scoffed at the look on her face.

"Ha! Why do you look so surprised? Seeing as you showed up here dressed like this. You must know by now. Why else would you break the disguise you've built over twenty years."

She was visibly upset by this. In her eyes, for just a split second, I could see the pain that my words had caused. I half expected her to cry, but just as quickly as it appeared, it faded away.

*"*I wasn't going to give her a chance to speak. It was clear to me whose side she was on.

"You played the part of the caring mother so well for so many years. But what did you do when I needed you the most? You

continued to side with them. You reported your brother to the police and almost got him killed."

"Police!?" echoed Maria in shock and horror. *"Yes, the police, Maria. My dearest mother almost got her brother arrested,"* I replied turning to look at her. I had tried my best to keep Maria out of this even back then, but this woman had to bring the

mess right to her doorstep.

I turned back to my mother and continued.

"you knew better than to do that. You knew that the police would have handed him straight over to Churchill and yet you still did that. Have you no heart?"

And then my mother finally spoke with condescension and self-righteousness that made my stomach turn.

"Oh please, Jaly. If I hadn't done what I had done, you would be a convicted felon like that rat you were running around with."

I was furious! Was she actually trying to justify her actions?

*"That 'Rat' was the only one among you with the courage to tell the **truth**! All he wanted was to find them! He wanted to save all of you cowards."*

"I put up with your stupidity for long enough. What you were doing wasn't trying to set anyone free. He was trying to blow up someone's property!" she replied.

"Blow up!" Maria echoed once more, growing ever more concerned about what was happening.

"You have no proof of that! He never wanted to hurt anyone and you know that!"

"They found enough explosives in the man's car to blow up a house! Did you expect me to let you keep running around with someone so dangerous?"

"That was planted to frame him. All of you have been using that poor man as a scapegoat for years!"

"Then how do you explain the explosion at the prison Jaliya!!!?" my mother shouted, her voice shrill and full of pain.

"…. explosion???" I said, my voice fading to a whisper, *"What explosion? He would never…."*

"He escaped last year and has been on the run ever since. For heaven's sake, Jaliya, do you hear yourself?!"

I stood in stunned silence. I knew enough to know that she was lying but not to know what the truth was. A few seconds passed in silence till Maria finally broke the silence.

"What on earth is going on here, Mama Jaliya? First, your daughter shows up at my door in the middle of the night and spends half the morning sobbing uncontrollably, acting like a mad woman. Then you show up at my door and start a screaming match talking about the police, bombs,

and terrorists!? Either you tell me what's going on or both of you leave right now!"

Both my mother and I looked at Maria.

"Go on, Jaliya," my mom spoke, *"tell your friend the real reason you had to leave your father's house. Seeing as she is the only person on the planet who would take you in, you at least owe her an explanation."*

Mother's taunting was cruel, but she was right. But then again I didn't know the truth. The fact that my mother knew where I was meant that *they* knew where I was that much I was sure of. On the other hand, why had my mother come alone? It made no sense.

"If I tell Maria now," I thought to myself, *"and it turns out that there is no connection between my mother and them, then I will lose the one person that has never lied to me or judged me.*

Then I realized something. If my mother knew the truth, there was no way she would be saying all this in front of Maria. It was either carelessness or ignorance. She probably only had a few pieces of the puzzle just like me. I needed to find out what she knows and perhaps this was the only chance I would get. My mother had made it seem like I was a spoiled and ungrateful child throwing a needless tantrum. As far as Maria was concerned, that was all that this was. Mother knew exactly what she was doing and probably thought that I would back down because of Maria. I didn't want her involved in this, but now that that choice had been made for me, there was no way I was backing down.

A Wandering Soul

It was a few weeks before our Senior 6 finals and the stress was on. Our school had an upstanding reputation to uphold and every student was constantly reminded of it.

I, on the other hand, wasn't interested in revising and cramming like a slave and spent most of my time dozing off as the teachers went on and on, trying to re-fit two years' worth of education into these poor, exhausted, and stressed-out students. I loved school for the freedom it gave me from my parents but the endless hours of cram work drove me mad. Don't get me wrong. I wasn't a slacker by any means! I was the best student in my class, so I didn't feel the need to crunch. After all, I'd been studying for this for 6 years.

One day after another uninspiring school lunch, I walked out of the dining hall towards the school's massive green courtyard. The courtyard was the thing I loved most about the place. The yard was surrounded on three sides by two classroom blocks and an administrative block. It was split into four square plots, outlined by cobblestone footpaths that had all but crumbled into dust. The grasses and weeds had begun to claim them all and I had observed this beautiful process for the 6 years I was there.

Each of the sections had a lush green carpet of grass, moss, and clovers with the odd blackjack weed that had escaped the custodian's watchful eye. I loved the shaded canopy that the trees dotted around the yard provided, and I spent as much time as I could underneath their shade.

It was there, under the dappled light of these trees, that I met the boy that would be my ruin, and his name was Anthony.

Anthony was a tall, dark-skinned sporty lad with a strange accented way of talking. His thick accent took nothing away from how articulate and well-spoken he was but I could never place where in the country it was from. I had seen him around the school a few times but had never really spoken to him until then.

Maria and I were close throughout school and had the same classes together every year. That afternoon we had found a comfy spot in the yard so she could revise like every other serious student, and so I could pretend to be revising with her. After a few minutes, I heard a group of students walk into the courtyard quarter directly behind ours. The tree was between us and the students on the other end didn't seem to see us there.

The group talked for a while about politics and

current affairs, and I didn't pay them any mind. At some point, the conversation turned to the ridiculous examination system of Uganda, throwing words like, "ludicrous" and "completely useless" at the topic. My interest was piqued!

Maria seemed to have been listening in on the conversation for much longer than I had and shot me a knowing glance.

"Jaliya, don't even think about it. We've already talked about this"

And we talked about it, a lot! The number of times I fell on Maria's bed after another exhausting evening prep, threatening to just drop out, were too many to count. After suffering through the mentally numbing classes and the teachers that cared more about our grades than us, I would spend my time reading all the books I wanted to or in a debate with a classmate about anything and everything. The only thing that had stopped me from dropping out was the fear of my parents, and when that failed, Maria was a constant voice of reason. She had convinced me to stay in school and fulfill all righteousness. But just because I had agreed to stick with it, doesn't mean my thoughts and feelings on the matter had changed.

"Oh, come on, you can't stop me from going over there. It can't be helped. You and I both know I was just pretending to read this book anyway,"

I set the book down and dusted the grass cuttings of my dark blue uniform skirt. Then I added with a chuckle,

"Maybe I might even learn something for once. Or better yet, convince them to think more productively."

She laughed and went back to her book knowing full well that I had never convinced anyone of anything. I took her silence as a go-ahead and made my way toward the group.

"...that's my whole point, Timo!" one of the five members of the group said. I recognized her as Judith, a girl I had sat next to the year before though I had never said a word to her in my life. I decided it was best to stay silent and listen to where the conversation was going before I spoke.

"How exactly does regurgitation of information prove that we have learned anything?" This time it was Mukasa who spoke. He was another classmate I had barely talked to outside of class.

"But Mukasa, your father is a teacher. You, of all people, should see how foolish this argument is. Are we supposed to remain illiterate?" Ronald added. And again, he was another classmate I recognized but had never spoken to.

The only member of the group I didn't recognize joked, *"So, they throw information at our faces and expect what to happen? Does your mother use Pythagoras'*

theorem as she mingles posho (maize meal)?"

The group burst into laughter and even Mukasa had to admit it. *"Naye Tony, you have no shame!"* And the laughter and debate continued.

It appears they hadn't noticed me, and I was a little relieved. Ashamed at how boldly I had walked over to a group of people I had essentially ignored the entire year was a little rude, even for me. I knew my people skills were bad, but not this bad.

"Jaliya, what do you think?" It was the one Mukasa had called Tony.

I leaned trying to look past Mukasa, who I had been standing behind.

"Is the stress HM (headmaster) is putting us through to get a so-called education worth the sleepless nights and ulcers?" he added.

I hadn't noticed until that point that the group was standing in a circle around him. I was a bit reluctant to say anything, but I could never pass up a chance to give my opinion on such a matter. I made my way passed Mukasa, Judith, and two more people I recognized as being from the class below me.

When I got to the middle of the circle, I was standing before Tony who looked and acted like the leader of the group. It was odd that I didn't recognize him if that was the case, but I decided to brush it off and ask later. I was given the chance to speak my mind, and I was way more excited than I should have been.

I placed my hands on my hips and rolled my eyes. *"I think it's utter nonsense...."* Tony smiled at me as I continued.

".... that you are all so close but still so clueless. Neither the teachers nor heavy workloads are the problem. The problem is that the education system was made for a world that is dead and gone. Sure 50 years ago being able to memorize and recite information word for word was helpful. And being punctual, well-dressed, and competent at rudimentary problem-solving was and still is a necessity. What these people don't realize is that that system was meant to train clerks and technicians to serve as assistants for the colonialists. And the paper you get at the end of that journey is all they needed to ensure that you were worth your weight in posho. Why would you need to know all of the geometrical postulates by heart when computer models replaced such jobs years ago? A look at the high unemployment rates is all you need to see that that paper is useless. But alas, the world still needs it."

Tony clapped as I finished and the smile on his face had turned into a horrid grin showing all 38 of his teeth. I was proud of myself until I saw that expression and almost jumped out of my skin. I didn't know a human being could make such a face.

"I knew you would agree with me on this one. That was exactly what I was trying to explain to your friends over here."
Then he reached out his hand and shook mine.
"I'm Anthony, by the way. But you can call me Tony. I've heard a lot about you from your classmates.

So nice to finally meet the legendary Jaliya."

Friends? I wouldn't have called them that. I was still questioning whether his expression from a few seconds ago was a hallucination but the part about me having a reputation on the other hand wasn't shocking.

"Jaliya, Tony just arrived today. He is from another school and moved to Kampala just this week. He's sitting his finals with us." Judith squeaked from behind me.

It wasn't unusual for students to sit their finals at another school. Although changing schools during the month of finals was something I hadn't heard of before. He was probably from a non-accredited institution. Probably a polytechnic institute. That would explain his apparent disdain for the formal education system. As I turned these thoughts over in my head, Tony shot me a knowing glance and cleared up my suspicions.

"From the look on your face, you seem to have figured me out already. At the risk of sounding pretentious, I'll call my education unconventional. I've been homeschooled for most of my life. My parents think just like you."

"So how come you're here?" I asked, still unsure of his story.

"You said it yourself, the world needs that paper!" he said, shrugging his shoulders. We both laughed, and I firmly shook his hand.

"Nice to meet you, Tony."

I then turned to the group behind me.

"So, what have you guys been saying behind my back? Nothing bad, I hope."

"Nothing that isn't true," Mukasa grinned, letting me know that they had indeed been saying some untrue things.

Judith enthusiastically pulled my arm towards her and pointed at my face. Her hand was so close to my eye that I was sure she would poke it.

"Didn't I tell you, Tony? You are totally the same. You could be twins!"

At that moment I remembered why I never talked to Judith. She was as jumpy as a baby goat and even louder than one! Anthony nodded in agreement,

"I'm glad I've found like-minded people on the first day. I had no hope in our schools but you are all proving me wrong. I had created a club so I could be around people that thought like me. Who knew when I would find people that were big thinkers!? It's so rare in our society!"

"I know right?" Judith added. *"It's no wonder this country never goes anywhere. We are all so content being distracted by the mundane and simple and never stopping to look at the bigger picture. It's infuriating!"*

We all looked at her shocked. Judith didn't look like the kind of girl that thought so deeply. The group laughed like we were thinking the same thing.

"Hey Tony, Jaliya, Judith, we should form a club like the one Tony had. Maybe we could share ideas and have some deep discussion during breaks!" Edward suggested. He was now as excited as Judith.

"Yeeesss," she called in a high-peached screech. *"Please, Tony. What was your club's name? We could be an extension of it."*

"It's called the Golden Dragonfly. And of course, we can form a club!"

Just then the bell rang signaling the end of the lunchtime break. Tony told us to meet in the same spot for the first club meeting the next afternoon. Judith, Mukasa, and the other two went on to their classes, and I turned to go find Maria so we could head back to class.

"Hey Jaliya," Tony called. I turned to look at him, and he gave me another strange smirk. *"See you around."*

I chill went down my spine. What was that smile? I shook it off and went to find Maria. I might not like school, but I didn't want to be late for class.

The next day all the suspicion I had towards Tony had faded. The way all the other kids seemed to follow him convinced me that it was all in my head. He was a natural-born leader and charismatic. Though he had his own very strong opinions, he never made anyone feel bad for disagreeing with him but instead actually encouraged us to share opposing sentiments and let the facts and logic decide who was right.

Though I wasn't into politics before meeting them, more focused on my immediate surroundings and the things I had read about, I found a place in the Golden Dragonfly Club that fed my love for probing discussions. Tony soon became like a big brother to the group. It was almost as if he could read minds, especially mine. As the days went on and exams began, The Golden Dragonfly meetings never slowed. On several occasions, a teacher or even the headmaster tried to disband our discussions, but we always found a way to meet and talk. Whether it was in the courtyard or behind one of the classroom blocks, we became more dedicated to our club than we were to anything else.

The club grew from six to over twenty in a span of 7 days. One of the things that was demanded of all club members was secrecy about what was spoken in our meetings. This seemed a little strange to me at first, seeing how Tony also encouraged us to grow the club. But the more people joined, the less we were encouraged to talk to non-club members.

This in particular re-awakened my suspicion of Tony's true intentions. I had continued to brush it off, enjoying the feeling of belonging that the club brought me, until one day, Tony pulled me aside and cautioned me about talking to Maria.

We had all finished our lunch earlier than everyone else as we always did, so we could have time for our club meetings before the bell rang. As I made my way to our meeting spot in the yard with Judith, Anthony called out to me from behind.

"Jaliya, wait a bit. I need to talk to you."

I let Judith go ahead and walked back toward Tony.

"Yes, Anthony what's up?" I asked, a little concerned.

"I've been seeing you with a certain girl since I arrived here, her name is...," snapping his hand in the air as he often did when trying to remember something.

"Are you talking about Maria?" I asked. *"Ah, yes! That's the one,"* he said, smiling. The smile quickly turned into a scowl.

"You need to stop spending so much time with her," he said in a serious tone.

The quick change in expression caught me off- guard. Sensing my shock, his face melted back into a charming and concerned look.

"You are turning out to be one of the brightest members of the Golden Dragonflies. There is a future we can build together as a team. We are just a small club now, but after exams, that is going to quickly change. Maria is not one of us and won't understand what we are trying to accomplish. She doesn't share our vision. As your friend, I'm only looking out for you and your future. You are going to be great and need to focus more on what you can do for not just the club, but for our nation."

Before I could process what he had said, he placed his hand on my shoulder, gave me a reassuring nod, and started toward the courtyard waving at other students as he passed by.

What did he mean by *"future"*? As far as I was concerned, this was a fun extra circular activity. I didn't know what to make of that event and never told Maria about it either. I thought about leaving the club after that but in my mind, any weirdness from him would be short-lived as I would probably never see any of these people after the exams were done and the term ended. For now, I could enjoy the company of people that seemed to appreciate my opinions. The feeling of belonging was too good to give up.

After the exams were done and we began packing for home, Tony called the Golden Dragonfly members for our final meeting. Since we couldn't meet as we usually did in the yard, we used one of the empty classrooms instead.

The desks had been piled in the back, the windows were closed, and on the chalkboard were the remnants of the final message the teacher had left.

I didn't pay much attention to what Tony was saying for the first half of the meeting. His voice faded into the background as I realized that this was the end of my high school career. It hadn't hit me until then and the memories of all I had gotten to experience came flooding back. As I was in the middle of a moment, realizing how much I had grown as a person, Mukasa elbowed me in the ribs, pulling me back into reality.

"Jaliya, pay attention."

Mukasa had caught on early to my habit of drifting off and made it his job to keep me present during Tony's speeches which I never really paid attention to. I honestly don't know if I was grateful or hated him for this.

Tony stood tall in the center of a circle, surrounded by 20 or so students. He looked less like a confident young man and more like a pompous peacock, and I had to stop myself from laughing. I pressed myself to listen with a straight face. After all, I wasn't going to see him again so we could at least end on good terms before I put all his eeriness behind me. His voice filled the classroom, bouncing off the walls and creating a slight echo.

"Up until this point, we have been mere secondary school students with big ideas. We've spent hours openly discussing the diseases that plague our nation, and the evil that runs deep in its veins. Now the time has come for us to act upon our words,"

Was this a campaign speech or something? Everyone in the crowd was empoisoned by his speech, taking in every word like thirsty chickens that had been in the sun all day.

"This guy would make a great politician," I whispered to Mukasa.

"Shhhh, listen" he scolded, as Tony went on. I rolled my eyes at him and did as he said.

"Injustices are going on beyond these walls that we have been made blind to. Our ears

are covered and we can't hear the cries of mothers as they weep for their children. You are here today because you can look past the veils, look beyond the painted horizon, and dream up a better future for this land. Blood is the currency with which we buy our freedom, and this nation is bankrupt."

Where did that come from? Caught off guard by his sudden intensity, we all began to murmur among ourselves. He then looked at the ground in front of him and with the heel of his shoe, scratched a line into

the dusty floor. Then he looked up smiling.

"I know this started as a fun club for friends that happen to have the same interests. I know that I probably won't see most of you again, so you are welcome to take the memories we have together and walk away. For those that choose to stay, I can promise that the things I am going to tell you will shatter your world and break your hearts. I promise you tears and pain. But I can also promise that those words will give you the chance to turn the dreams that we dreamt up together into a reality. Those that cross this line are free to never look back."

The murmuring continued as all of us were thoroughly confused and concerned. A lot of the students were scared of what he was saying and more of how he was saying it. One by one student after student stood up, said their goodbyes to all of us, and left the classroom. Tony gave each one a big hug and bid them adieu.

Soon only Judith, Mukasa, Tony, and Myself were left in the room.

"I always knew there was a purpose to all this. You planned this all out, didn't you? To inspire us and to push us to reach our full potential." Judith was as excited as ever and as usual, fully placed her faith in Tony.

"My God Tony! I don't know what is going on, but I don't think I want to miss this one. That was intense!" Mukasa said pulling a chair from the back of the room and staking a seat set to Anthony.

So, Judith stayed because of faith and Mukasa stayed out of curiosity. Everything in me told me to leave that room, but to this day I don't know what made me stay.

"You are weird, you know that," I said laughing. *"But, it's hard to not want to hear what comes after this."* I walked to the back, pulled up three more chairs and we all sat down in a half circle.

Once we had settled into our seats, Tony finally spoke. *"I'm not surprised that the ones this all began with are the ones that stayed."*

He sighed deeply as he stood up, reached into his pocket, pulled something out, and then sat back down. It was a folded piece of paper. As he slowly unfolded it, tears began to stream down his face.

"Well," I thought to myself, *"here is my proof that he is unstable."*

We watched in silence as he unfolded what turned out to be a picture, and he held it out for us to see. It was a picture of a girl that looked no older than any of us. She had beautiful long hair braided in four neat cornrows that fell to her shoulders. Her dark hair contrasted with her bright white smile. She wore what I assumed was a uniform but I couldn't make out what school it was from. The strange part was that the picture looked to be decades old.

After we had all had a good look at it, Tony spoke again. *"This is Nairo. She is...was my sister. We grew up in a village up north with my uncle and our sister. Almost 20 years ago, she was taken to the city by a man promising her a better life."*

I can still remember the look of horror on all our faces. The contrast between the light-hearted conversations and the things Tony said that day left us all in shock. None of us could have anticipated this. Human trafficking and a possible murder were the last things on our minds.

"Everyone said it was just another case of human trafficking. But I don't buy that one bit. Nairo was just another victim of a story we have heard countless times," he added, tears streaming

down his face. *"When we tried to get justice for her, the police told us that there was nothing they could do. We went to every politician we could, and all of them turned us away. No one cared to search for her before, and now that she was dead, they cared even less."*

The pain in his voice was like a hot knife through our hearts. It was as if we were watching a wound that had just begun to heal being pulled open. *"Back then, I didn't know why no one cared. I couldn't understand why those that had been called to protect and serve treated us like we don't matter. Now I know it's because we have never mattered to them at all. To these politicians and bureaucrats, you are nothing but a vote. You've lived all your lives with the danger of trafficking, murder, rape, and violence as a background song. You've been in the safety and comfort of your parents' homes. But for how long will you let the streets run red with the blood of the innocent? For how long will you be blind to the reality that yesterday it was Nairo, but tomorrow it could be your mother, sister, or even you? Will you continue living your lives as if Nairo's did not matter? If you and I don't do something about this, no one else will."*

I felt tears begin to roll down my cheek. How horrible that must have been for a young boy to go through. After a few more minutes of this speech, he wiped his face and reached into his other pocket. He then pulled out what looked like business cards. One side was black with a gilded, Golden Dragonfly and the other was white with something scribbled on it. He folded three of the cards and handed each of us. He told us not to open them until we had given ourselves time to think about what he had told us. And that soon, we would have all the answers to our questions. I don't remember what was said after that and the rest of the

day was a blur.

That evening at home, I lay in my bed with the Golden Dragonfly card in my hand. I watched as the light danced across the wings of the gilded insignia and chased the several trains of thought that run through my head. On the one hand, my suspicions about Anthony were right. He wasn't a normal boy. I had known something was wrong with him from day one and in my hand was my confirmation. The things he said weren't normal. Neither was it normal for a high school boy to carry around such expensive-looking business cards for an after-class club. Anthony had been holding all this back and I wondered what more he was hiding.

Then I thought about the picture of his sister. She looked just like a normal girl. She looked like me. The thought that she was murdered in cold blood was one I could not stand. It infuriated me to think such an innocent-looking person was ripped so coldly from this world.

I cried for most of the night as my emotions jumped from sadness to anger, to despair and hopelessness. The last thing I thought about before I eventually fell asleep was the pain and anguish I saw that day in Tony's eyes. The sound of his quivering voice as he handed the picture to me was seared into my mind.

What a great actor he was.

Familiar Shadows

It was a few weeks into my form six vacation and all I could think about were Tony's words and that black card. I had spent every waking moment thinking about his words and debating on if I should reach out to him or stay as far away from the matter as possible.

One evening as I was chopping vegetables for my mother, I began talking to myself.

"Should I read what's on the card? Is that girl's death any of my business?...But she didn't deserve to die the way she did...what does that have to do...with me? Can I truly stop something so terrible from happening to anyone else? But Jaliya, do I think I can bear the world's problems on my shoulders? But this isn't about me...."

"Are you okay Jaliya?" my mother asked, placing her hand on my shoulder.
I jumped and gazed into her eyes for a moment. Was I really talking out loud? I assured her I was fine

and immediately went back to my room.

Deep down I wanted to believe that his strange behavior was perhaps due to the trauma and pain of losing his sister. That must have been such a horrible experience for him. Maybe that's what messed him up. I couldn't imagine having to go through something like that at such a young age. Though I had no siblings, I had people that I counted on and if anything like that happened to Maria or my mom, I'd be devastated.

As I lay on my bed that night, my fear and distrust had slowly grown into a burning curiosity. The more that I thought about it, the more one thing stood out. The timelines made no sense! I knew Tony was a little older than us, but the math didn't fit.

If his sister had disappeared 20 years ago then how old was he when she went missing? He remembered it all so well, so I guessed he couldn't have been any younger than ten. But that would make him at least 30! If that were true, it would explain why he stood out so much. The way he spoke, his mannerisms, and the way he carried himself reminded me more of my dad or one of the male teachers than it did a boy in his late teens or early 20s.

I tried to look his family up on the internet but then realized I didn't even know Tony's last name. I
messaged Maria to ask her and she also didn't know.

Logging into our class's chat room, I sent out a message asking, if anyone knew, but.... nothing. None of them knew anything about him. Not where he was from or what his parents did. No one knew if he lived close to the city or up-country. I couldn't even find one person that had the same classes as him. We had all assumed he was in another class and never asked. Some students outright denied ever meeting an Anthony!

One as I was doing some more digging on the matter and trying to find anything I could on the mystery that was Tony, I heard a voice outside my window.

My room was parallel to the perimeter wall with only a meter-wide space between the wall and my window. People had always used this space as a sort of secret hideout to have conversations they didn't want anyone else to hear. What they did not know, is that I could hear every single word.

I, a professional at minding my own business, always tried my best not to listen in. I usually plugged my headphones into my ears and played some music to distract myself from whatever they were saying. For the past few days, my mom had been using the secret spot more than she ever did and it was getting harder and harder to ignore her. She had only done this when she was planning a surprise or talking to her girlfriends about her personal life so at first, I didn't care. I had other things to worry about anyway.

This was the fourth night in a row and she would talk for no less than two hours each time. I began to worry it had something to do with me since she and my father were constantly on my case about university and eventually, my curiosity got the better of me. Against my better judgment, I decided to unplug my earphones and listen in just to make sure I was in the clear.

I slowly crawled up to the window from my bed, took out my earphones, and pressed my head to the wall next to the window. I couldn't see my mum but I could see her shadow in the gap between the wall and my curtains. She spoke in a low voice, not quite a whisper, which made it hard to hear what she was saying. And no matter how I tried, I couldn't hear the voice on the other end of the line.

"Are you sure that Tony and Anthony are the same person? I hope you actually checked the school records this time"
"…………"

"No, I don't doubt you. But why would he go as far as joining my daughter's high school? He is a grown man! How does that happen? What kind of school lets a grown man in…?"
"…………………"

"I know I should be happy he is alive. But you and I both know what this means. He of all people should know what that means. He knows how much danger he is putting us all in. I knew he was mad, but this is too much."
"………..."

"We have all sacrificed a lot to be here. I can't allow this boy's foolishness to get another person killed."
"…………"

"Do you at least know where he has been this whole time?"
"..................."

"so you're telling me that he broke out of prison? How in the world....you know what, I don't want to know. Does Churchill know about this?"
"..............."

"This is not good. I have no idea what he is planning but I will not let him drag that innocent child into this."

She hung up and let out a deep sigh, then walked calmly toward the back door and into the house. I let out a breath I hadn't realized I was holding and fell back onto my bed.

"What did I just hear?" I whispered to myself.
"Is she talking about Tony? It has to be the same guy. I knew something wasn't right with him. How does Mom know him in the first place? *"And what does Uncle Churchill have to do with either of them?"*

The mention of Uncle Churchill was what struck fear into me. I had only had a few interactions with him when I was a little girl, but I knew enough to stay as far into the shadows as possible when it came to him.

Matthew Churchill was a wealthy businessman and politician whom my father had worked with closely. He had run for public office a long time ago but then moved to fund the politicians instead. Churchill was a shrewd and wicked man who also happened to be my mother's uncle. Everyone called him Uncle Churchill regardless of relation. To those in his protection, he gave favor and wealth but to those that had opposed him, a fate worse than death. My parents had distanced themselves from him after a scandal involving the disappearance of a young woman a little after I was born but stayed in contact for a few years eventually cutting him off completely. At least that's what I thought. So why was my mom mentioning him now?

The next day at breakfast, my mother kept looking at me with darting glances which made me incredibly uncomfortable. She had been doing this the past few days, but I had ignored it. I would have preferred to skip breakfast altogether that morning but I wasn't about to give my father another reason to scold me. Obviously, his only concern was my results and when they were coming out.

"As if I have any power over that!" I retorted over and over. But did he listen? No.

This morning I was more focused on my mother and her strange behavior. She was in her usual get-up, a large shapeless batik dress, with a head wrap to match. I couldn't, for the life of me, believe that what I heard last night came from her! She seemed so harmless and passive. To think she would get involved with Churchill was unbelievable. I had never really thought of my mother as someone with a controversial past, but the look on her face was as if something was coming back to haunt her.

I avoided my mother for the rest of the week. Paranoid that she knew I had overheard her that night; I was too anxious to think clearly. I desperately needed to get out of the house and that weekend decided to head over to Maria's place.

"Come on, Jaliya!" was Maria's response when I told her about Tony. I couldn't tell her everything about Churchill but I couldn't not talk about how weird his story was. Desperate to get some of it off my chest, I told her about the club meetings and the last day, leaving out the part about his dead sister. I did not like lying to my best friend but even I wouldn't believe me if I told the whole truth.

"So, you want me to believe that the leader of your weird club somehow came out of nowhere.?" she continued.

I rubbed my brow in frustration.

"I'm not telling you to believe me, I'm simply stating things as I see them. Tony is bad news." She was right, this all sounded

ridiculous. I regretted even opening my mouth. What proof could I give to my claims? I had nothing on him, except for that very damming conversation I overheard. But that's a secret remember. How frustrating!

"He is probably just one of those super private people. I wouldn't be surprised if he was one of those radical internet haters with how weird his other beliefs are."

"But that's just the thing. How would he be so caught up on current affairs if he didn't believe in the internet? And what weirdo doesn't use social media? Even my dad does!"

"Jaly, jumping to conclusions and accusing your friend of some wickedness because he has a few weird habits isn't fair. Especially when he confided in you about his views. I agree he did give off some weird vibes. The guy always seemed to know way too much about everything. Not to mention how old he looked and sounded! But there is no way he is a 30-year-old man."

I watched as she jumped from sentiment to sentiment. The mental gymnastics she was performing to try and make sense of this was impressive. After a while, she went silent and looked at me very seriously.

"You need to stay clear of whatever this is Jaliya. I'm sure it's nothing but I know you. Once you get curious you won't listen to anyone. You're like a cat. We all know what happens to curious cats."

I didn't like being compared to a cat but it's not like she was wrong. My curiosity had gotten me into some problems in the past which is why I always tried so hard to mind my own business. But this was not something that I could just ignore. If for some reason this was all connected to his sister's murder and Churchill had something to do with it, then it was already my business.

When I got back from Maria's place that evening, I looked at the folded black card on my dresser. I leaned against my door and stared intently at it, begging it to give me the answers to all the questions in my mind. The more I stared at it, the more obnoxious and contemptuous it looked. The Golden Dragonfly embossed onto the sea of black seemed to stare back at me. Honestly, it made me nauseous to think about all that Tony had said when he handed these cards to us. The memories of his deranged smile and pained eyes fought in my mind. I couldn't tell which one was the real Tony.

I walked to the dresser, picked it up and threw it into the drawer, and slammed it shut. Thinking about all this was beyond frustrating.

I changed my clothes and got straight into bed. Sleep was the goal but my brain clearly hated me and kept dragging my thoughts back to the whole situation. I had to reason with myself. I had to have had more sense than that. This wasn't some James Bond movie or murder mystery novel! This was the real world. And I was way in over my head.

"I know I don't have much going on in my life but this is not the kind of excitement I need. If there turns out to be nothing to it, then I've already lost too much of my peace to this and it would be best to let it go. And if there is something to it, then letting it go is still the best option. And that's the end of that"

Except it wasn't! My brain was never one to listen to reason and the haunting thoughts continued. I decided to stop trying to fight it, trusting that I would fall asleep eventually. I stared at my ceiling waiting for the sweet relief of sleep. After hours of steeping in a stew of thoughts, I so desperately wanted nothing to do with, I checked the time. 4:00 am!

I should have known that that's just not how a Jaliya works. As I went further and further down the rabbit hole, my head shot up when I realized something. I might have known little about Tony, but I knew even less about my mom.

I knew she wasn't the first woman my father had married but I had never been told what happened to his first wife. Everyone acted like she never existed. I had suppressed memories of a woman when I was really little that I could never place, but she wasn't my mother. I had always thought that the woman was a maid or something. If there was ever a time for insignificant details to become significant, it was now.

"Wow, Jaliya, what next? Your mom isn't your mum? You need mental help!"

Laughing the idea off, I decided to get myself a glass of water and made my way down the hall as quietly as possible. I got my glass of water and a little midnight snack then headed back to my room. As I walked back from the kitchen, through the living room towards my bedroom, I saw that the study lights were on. The study was in the room right after mine, so I hadn't noticed it when I went to the kitchen.

"Who on earth is in there at this hour?"

The only person that used the study other than me was my father and it couldn't have been him. Not at that hour. I could still hear his snoring rumble across the hallway. I walked as silently as I could towards the slightly ajar study door to get a better look.

When I finally got a look through the crack, my eyes grew wide. It was my mother! She was on the floor surrounded by albums, envelopes, files, random papers, and all sorts of other documents. I watched as she flipped through album after album until she eventually threw the last one to the ground in frustration. She seemed to give up on whatever it was she was searching for and began to carefully rearrange the books onto the shelf. When she

was done, it was as if she was never there.
Locks and Keys

The following morning when my parents had both left and the house was quiet, I took the first chance I got to head into the study to try and find out what my mother was looking for.

I made my way to the study and shut the door behind me. The study had large floor-to-ceiling shelves that covered every wall with my father's desk in the middle of the room facing the door. The desk sat on top of an old cow skin rug and the red leather and velvet chair that my father had custom-made gave the room a luxurious yet haunting aura. There were no windows, so the fluorescent lights had to be left on all the time. The shelves were lined with books on just about any topic. From law to sports, to history. My father was very proud of his collection. I remember spending hours seated on the red-carpeted floors reading books from the African Writer's Series that my father had bought for me when I was about thirteen. Those were the only novels I was ever permitted to touch outside of school. A love for books and dark study corners seemed to be all the three of us had in common.

I had barely entered the study for the past six years since I was in boarding school and had missed the long lazy afternoons spent huddled up in a corner reading. I took in every detail of the intricate but timeless craftsmanship of the shelves and the musty smell of the old red carpet that lined the floors.

With a deep breath, I walked toward the shelf with the albums. There were two rows of albums fairly close to the ground on the shelf behind the desk. They were organized from oldest to newest and my mother had been looking through the older albums. I reached for a few of them and began to flip through the pages. My anxiety soon turned to disappointment as page after page proved to be photos I had seen countless times before. Pictures of our family through the years that I felt no connection to. The smiles were so obviously fake and plastered on for the camera: my first day of school, all the sports days that only my mom attended, birthday parties with no friends, Christmases with no relatives, and so forth. What a bleak picture they painted of my childhood. Nothing like the lazy golden afternoons I had remembered.

I made it through all the albums on the first row and placed them all back onto the shelf. I then looked at those on the second row, but it was the same story. More photos I was emotionally detached from. I decided not to waste my time and put them right back. I looked up, scanning the room for anything that seemed even the slightest bit out of place. Did I know what exactly I was looking for? No. But I looked anyway.

After searching in vain for a while, I threw myself into my father's desk chair, frustrated. *"There's nothing here!"* There was nothing on the shelves and if there was, maybe my mother had found it. What a waste of time!

I folded my hands on the desk, rested my head on them as I accepted the futility of my efforts, and contemplated what to do next. Looking at the items on my father's desk all I saw was: an award for something he probably didn't do, a stapler placed atop a neatly arranged stack of papers and documents, a few empty envelopes, and a rouge pen.

There wasn't much to look at as my father only used this space when he was reading or finishing up something he had failed to do at his office. As I stared blankly at the stack of papers, I noticed the document on the top of the stack looked slightly whiter than the rest. My father was very particular about the brand of printer paper he used and hated stark white sheets, opting for warm-toned paper instead. There was another strange thing about that document. A black and gold insignia of the initials *'MC'* with what looked like tiny dragonflies encircling the initials.

"I've seen this somewhere before," I thought. I tried to think of where I remembered it from, and a light bulb went off in my head.

There was only one man my father knew who was so full of himself that he would have custom stationery made!

"Uncle Churchill!"

I carefully lifted the stapler that was on the stack of documents and picked the document up praying that my sweaty hands wouldn't leave a mark. Looking it over, I noticed that it was five sheets of paper stapled together, each with the same insignia at the top left corner. I scanned over the contents of the cover letter and it was nothing special. Just a letter of invitation to an award event for the launch of a student fund or something along those lines.

One of Uncle Churchill's political tactics was to create funds for different demographics in an attempt to show that he cares for and gives back to the community. Of course, these fund launches were always conveniently scheduled around six months before the election season. What a farce! I rolled my eyes in disgust and threw the letter back onto the desk. After taking a few seconds to put my political opinions aside, I picked the document back up and looked through the rest of the pages. One thing was confirmed now, my father definitely had not severed ties with Churchill as he had claimed. Not surprising. Who in their right mind would give up such a lucrative partnership? Not to mention the fact that technically, it was his father-in-law. This was shocking but this can't have been what my mom was looking for. If it was, she would have already found it. Churchill and my father were connected through the work that they did but my mom stayed away from my father's political aspirations.

"So what are they both doing around Churchill? Where is the connection between Mother and Tony?! The answer had to be in this room, but where was it?!"

None of the other documents in the stack had Uncle Churchill's insignia on them so I placed the document back exactly where I had found it. I then thought to look through the drawers of the desk. The first had nothing but a stack of blank papers, a notepad, and a pen. The second was empty and the third was locked. I looked around for the key but couldn't find it. Of course.

"It has to be in their room."

I recalled that my father always kept important keys in a glass bowl in his room.

"But how on earth am I going to get that key?" I pondered my situation and genuinely considered giving up. But I had finally found something that promised an answer and up until now, all I had was questions. I had to know what was in that drawer!

After racking my head for a while, I had three possible plans of action. One, I could wait for my parents to get back and then find a way to sneak into their room and grab the key during supper. But there was no way this would work as I wasn't allowed anywhere near my parent's room after I had been caught trying to take money from my father's wallet a couple of years earlier. Not my proudest moment. If they so much as heard the door open, the jig was up!

Option two was to somehow convince the maid that I needed something from their room so she could use the spare key she had.

The third option was to try and pick their lock before they got home. Had I ever picked a lock before? No. But desperate times called for creative thinking, and I was desperate. The curiosity in me had grown from a silent whisper to a deafening scream. Unfortunately, this isn't that sort of book. I decided to go with option two.

Molly, the maid, and I were on cordial terms as she was still fairly new so she was my best bet. I made sure to leave everything in the study as I had found it, in case my father came back earlier than expected and went over to Molly's room.

"Yes please," she said after I knocked on her door.

"Uhhhh...Molly, it's me, Jaliya."

After a few seconds of rustling, she opened the door.

Molly was a stout, but well-built woman in her late 30s that always had a smile on her face. Other than the few unavoidable interactions we had, we never really spoke. She did her work and returned to her room, never lounging around in the living room, a habit that had gotten a few of the previous maids fired by my father. He was a very strict and uptight man that demanded the highest level of discipline from his workers. He required the maids to wear a uniform which was as ridiculous as it sounds. And there she was in the doorway, tucking her white and green striped button-down shirt with a pink frilly collar into the ankle-length jet-black pencil skit provided by my father's tailor. At least they didn't make her pay for that monstrosity. I tried my best to ignore the crime of fashion and set my mind to the task.

"Yes, dear how can I help you?" Molly asked again, still fiddling with the waistband and hem of her skirt and adjusting her collar.

"Ummm...I'm sorry to have to bother you," I said in the most innocent voice I could master. *"I need my admission papers from Mommy and Daddy's room to apply for something. It seems they will be back really late and I forgot to ask them before they left. Could*

you please help me and open their room for me? I promise it would take only a few minutes to get the information I need then I will put the documents right back."

I could see the skepticism in her eyes and for a moment I thought she saw right through my act. At least it wasn't all a lie.

"Are you sure you can't wait for them to come back?" she said with one brow lifted.

"yes…… but the truth is I don't want my father to know that I'm applying to this place."

"Why don't you want him to know?" I could hear the doubt in her voice growing and I knew that this had to be one of the most convincing performance of my life.

"Daddy doesn't want me to go to this school. He wants me to do a 'reasonable course'," I said looking down in shame. I then looked into her eyes and continued.

"But if I can get accepted and show him that I really want to go and that this is what I want then maybe he might let me do it. Molly, I can't spend my life living the dream that my father has for me. I just want the chance to do what I want with my life and pave my own paths. Do you see what I'm saying?"

I clasped her hands in mine as I spoke and a single tear rolled down my left cheek. Molly looked at me with sympathy, as if her heart was about to break.

"I know how you feel my girl. I lived my life according to what my parents wanted and look at me now. A degree and a master's but working as a maid."

I had to push back the shock at her sudden burst of emotions and keep her gaze. She took a few seconds to compose herself and clear her throat. Then she squeezed my hands and disappeared back into her room.

"You are right my girl. You deserve to live a life on your terms. That father of yours is a difficult man, but I've noticed that you can stand up for yourself."

She came out with the key and placed it in my hands. She clasped both my hands in hers. *"I don't know what dream it is that you have Jaliya, but don't let anyone take that away from you. Keep fighting like I always see you do."*

Molly's words were so heartfelt and genuine. I didn't know what felt worse, the fact that I had just lied straight through my teeth or my apparent reputation for insubordination. Either way, I had what I had come for and nodded, whipping the single tear

from my eye. She checked to make sure that no one had overheard us then gently shoved me towards the house.

"Go, quickly. Go get the documents and bring the key back to me. I won't tell anyone. But please, bring it back as quickly as possible. If

Mister finds out, I will be fired on the spot, and I can't afford to lose this job."

"Thank you so much, Molly," I said, shaking my head vigorously up and down. *"I promise I'll be right back."*

I looked at her once more and then turned to go back to the main house. As I walked I felt more tears stream down my face. *"Did I buy into my own act?"*

But this was not the time to pause and question myself, I pushed whatever it was down and kept going. I chucked as I whipped the tears off my face. *"Maybe I should consider being an actress!"*

Once I had opened my parent's bedroom door, I quickly located the clear glass bowl full of keys on my father's dresser. I carefully rummaged through it until I found one that looked like it would open the drawer. It wasn't that hard to locate as it was noticeably smaller than the others. I clutched it tightly just in case it dematerialized in my hand and then I made my way back to the study, closed the door behind me.

By some miracle of heaven, it was the right key and the drawer slid right open. Inside was a single envelope with Uncle Churchill's black and gold insignia on it. *"Bingo!"*

My heart began to beat in my ears as I plucked up the envelope in excitement. As I was about to open it I heard my father's car horn at the gate and my heart dropped. I quickly slammed the door shut and locked it. It was a mad dash for my parent's bedroom and I barely manage to throw the key back into the bowl, slam their door shut and lock it. Running to my room, I threw the envelope under my blanket and stated for Molly's quarters to return the key.

As I sprinted out the back door, I nearly crashed into my mother.

"Juliya who is chasing you?" she said, half amused and half annoyed by this unconventional welcome. I laughed uncomfortably as my fingers tightened around the spare bedroom key in my hand. She looked at me like I had gone mad and I manage to blurt out a proper greeting before shuffling past her and out of the house.

Things That Fly Must Fall

"You have to come back with me, Jaliya. You have no idea how much of a mess you've made."

My mother cut me off as I retold the events of the past few months. Her tone had completely changed. She had dropped all pretense of being a mother concerned for her daughter's wellbeing. I couldn't understand why she was so furious when it seemed like she had no right to be. She was the one that was keeping secrets this whole time!

"I have nothing to hide. You're the one trying to cover up a...."

She cut me off again. This time yelling furiously.

"JALIYA! Don't you say another word! You know nothing about any of this. You have no idea how much pain and suffering you have caused on this selfish self-righteous crusade of yours!"

I couldn't believe what I was hearing.

"Selfish crusade?! Who do you think you are? What right do you have to say anything when you quite literally have blood on your hands!"

What little restraint I had was gone. I could no longer hold back all the anger and disgust I felt and I didn't care who was in the room.

My mom paused for a moment. She had the sense to know that the direction this conversation was taking was not for Maria's ears.

"Maria," she spoke once more with concern, her eyes never parting with mine. *"Please could you give me and my daughter some time to speak in private?"*

Maria who was in shock and trying to process everything she had just learned snapped out of her trance.

"Yes. I'll give you both some time to talk."

As Maria walked out of her room she shot me a glance that said, *"What on earth have you done now Jaliya?"*

"Jaliya, what exactly did you find in the study that day?" my mother asked as soon as Maria had closed the door behind her.

"If you found what I fear you did; you probably hate me right now. But you have to tell me exactly what it is you found in that drawer otherwise a lot of people are going to get hurt."

A familiar fear filled her eyes as she spoke. It was the same fear I felt when I discovered what those envelopes hid.

I remembered walking to my room as fast as I could after I returned the key to Molly. I didn't dare lift my gaze fear of arousing any more suspicion than I already had.

When I finally got to my room I quickly locked the door behind me and let out a sigh of relief. I closed the window and drew my curtains before I reached for the envelope hidden under my blanket. When I finally had it in my hands I looked it over carefully, taking in every detail.

There was nothing really special about it save for Uncle Churchill's obnoxious initials plastered in bright blue ink on the top left corner. My mind raced with possibilities but truth be told I couldn't think of anything so important, it had to be kept under lock and key in the study.

I tried to be as gentle as possible as I opened the envelope but my excitement couldn't be contained. I turned the envelope upside down and violently shook its contents onto the floor and out flew a torrent of photographs and what looked to be handwritten letters. I carefully picked up the first photo, a black-and-white image of what looked to be a family. The date on the back was

October 5th, 1979, 31 years ago. It was taken under a mango tree outside of an old- looking house.

The photo was of three children, two girls, one boy, and two men. One of the men wore a kanzu and a hat and was seated on a short, wooden stool. His outstretched hand rested on an ornately carved cane that stood straight in the grass. He had a soft and relaxed look on his face which contrasted the look on the face of the man standing next to him. This man was slim and stood tall in his Mutema-style suit. His deep, sunken eyes gave him a cold and harsh look as if he was deeply disappointed in something.

The two girls were both dressed in long frilly white dresses covered in lace and sat in front of the man with their legs tucked to one side which was the traditionally appropriate way for a respectable lady to sit. Behind the man in the kanzu stood a boy that bore a strong resemblance to him. One of the boy's hands was placed on his shoulder and the other on the collar of his shirt, as if he was covering something.

I recognized one of the girls as my mother when she was younger, as I had seen a few photos of her from her childhood. She looked to be around ten at the time in this one. I didn't know much about my mother's family and was told that she was the fourth born of six children, three of whom had died before the age of 5. All I know about her living siblings was that she had a younger brother and an older sister. Seeing as my mother's life wasn't a topic free for discussion, I had never been told what became of them.

It all began to add up and I realized that I was holding a picture of my mother's family in my hands. The other two children in the photo had to be her two remaining siblings. The boy looked significantly younger than her, around 5 or six and the girl was definitely older than her. I had been kept in the dark about my family's history and never thought I would get such a clear glimpse into my mother's past.

This was a very emotional moment for me and I felt tears begin to well up in my eyes. However, this was not the time for sentimentality. I did my best to push them back as I felt my heart begin to ache. This was a pain I had learned to silence since I was a child and did so this time as well, placing the photo to the side.

When I picked up the second photo I could not believe my eyes. It was my mom again, this time much older and she was standing next to a man that looked more than familiar. Was that Tony?! When I flipped the photo over to check the date, April 6th', 1999, eleven years ago!

"This can't be right," I said to myself. I grabbed the final photo and it was a copy of the photo that Tony had shown us on the last day of school.

My ears began to ring, and the room began to spin as my eyes darted from photo to photo desperately looking for something to prove I was wrong. I studied each of the faces in the photos over and over but there they were, staring right back at me. My mother and that girl Tony had said was his sister were the two girls in the first photo. And then there he was. Tony was the boy in the photo. Were the three of the siblings?!

PART TWO

*"If you want to clean the land in secret, the noise
of the axe will give you away"*

-African Proverb-

***

Vanish in The Skies

Letter 1

Nairo to Talika

June 21, 1990

Dear Talika,

How have you been? You were so excited to start Form Four, and I hope that your studies are going well. I know it can get stressful, but I want to encourage you to keep going and aim for your Form Six. Unlike me, you have been allowed to do so, and I know you have the brains for it.

I'm sorry I wasn't able to see you this holiday. I know you must have looked forward to seeing me. I know that Uncle Churchill probably didn't explain the situation I have found myself in, and if he did, I'm not confident he told you the truth. I had to wait until school had started again so I could send this to you there because I knew that was the only way it would reach you. Please do me a favor and burn this letter once you have finished reading it, for what I am about to tell you might put you in danger. I want to apologize right now for dragging you into this mess, and I promise I would never put you in such danger unless it was absolutely necessary.

As I write this, I am hiding in the maid's room of my husband's house, hoping that I don't get caught. Yes, my sister, Uncle Churchill finally married me off. We all knew it was coming, but I had hoped it would be later rather than sooner.

Do you remember last year when Uncle Churchill came home with a certain young man from one of his party meetings? I know you remember that tall, dark, and uptight fellow, Charles. He was the one in the army green Kaunda suit and sharp brown shoes with his hair neatly packed in an afro. I remember how jealous you were of his hair because Uncle Churchill had made you cut yours for Christmas.

After I had served Uncle Churchill and his guest's tea that day, Uncle asked me to stay a while and chat with them. That was so terrifying. Uncle had warned us against saying anything to the guest beyond our greetings and would always answer on our behalf when we were asked anything. And then there was the fact that this was one of the party members! What was I supposed to say to them? I wanted nothing to do with politics, especially after what happened to our father.

Uncle Churchill went on and on about how well-mannered I am and how sharp and smart I am. All the while I was just sitting there, like one of the cups on the table. I spoke only to answer questions directly addressed to me and nodded along with whatever Uncle said the rest of the time. After a few hours of this torture, Charles finally left.

As I was heading off to the kitchen to help you prepare the food, Uncle Churchill called me back again and asked me what I thought of Charles. I found Charles to be silent, uptight, boring, long-winded, and harsh when he did eventually speak. He spoke only of work and party business and seemed to have no opinion on anything other than those two things. He also had a permanent scowl on his face as if he was always in the presence of an offensive smell. Of course, I couldn't tell Uncle Churchill any of this and simply said, *"I think he is a hard-working and focused man."* The mental gymnastics I had to do to get to that somewhat diplomatic answer were a stretch, I know, but I was not about to say anything to offend Uncle.

Over the next few weeks, we saw a lot more of Charles and I began to suspect that Uncle Churchill was up to something. I mean, he is always up to something, but I didn't know what it was this time. It couldn't be a political game to try and befriend a member of an opposite party to gain 'intel' as he had done in the past. Charles was a member of the same party. Then I thought it could be an internal struggle for the currently vacant seat of party chair. But Charles seemed to show no interest in it and they barely ever spoke about that matter. I also wondered why *I* always had to be there. I didn't have to wonder for too long as Uncle Churchill eventually made his true intentions known. It was about a week after you had left for school and Uncle Churchill was with Charles in the living room going over the same things they had talked over countless times. After Charles had finally left, Uncle Churchill called me back to the sitting room. I came in from the kitchen and knelt. He then told me that over the past few months, he had been testing Charles. I asked what exactly he was testing him for and he told me that he wanted to see if Charles would make a good husband for me. Oh my God, Talika! My heart stopped beating there and then. I asked him if he was serious and he was. He went on and on about how Charles was a good man with a solid head on his shoulders, how Charles came from a good family with a lot of land, houses, and property, and how it would be a blessing to be in such a family. As he spoke, it felt like I was falling deeper and deeper into an abyss. At some point, Uncle Churchill's words began to fade into the background and were replaced by a deafening ring in my ears.

"The wedding is in two weeks..."

Those were the words that threw me back into reality. I tried to protest asking why it had to be so soon and why I had to get married in the first place, but there was nothing to be done about it. And indeed, two weeks later, I found myself in the village chapel with Uncle Churchill, Charles' parents, and a priest. I couldn't even process what was going on. I simply stood there, looking dazed in the long white dress I had received for Christmas from Uncle Churchill. That wicked man had been planning this for a long time!

Before I knew it, I was walking into a large house in the capital with my suitcase in one hand and my shattered dreams in the other. It's been nearly two months and my life in this place has been torture. Though he is distant and crude, Charles isn't the worst person in the world. He does not mistreat me, but he isn't exactly warm and affectionate either. I barely see him because he leaves before the sun has risen and returns long after it has set. What surprises me the most is that somewhere along the way something happened and now I'm pregnant!

I've spent countless nights wondering how and why I ended up in this situation and I can't stomach any of my theories. I have a decent idea as to why Uncle Churchill arranged this marriage, and I'm almost certain there is something sinister going on. I've tried my best to stay out of my husband's business and have ignored the red flags as much as possible. His mysterious trips, the way he quickly hangs up the phone when I enter the room how he sends me out of the room when he receives a call. He also often has long meetings with his father and other men that go on for almost the whole day. It's beyond boring here but I'm not allowed to go outside the gate alone. They probably think I'd make a break for it, and they are not wrong. I spend my days wandering the hallways and compounds, or reading and sewing to keep myself busy. I also occasionally spend my afternoons with Charles's parents when they call for me. Now I have my child's life to think about. I don't think I can afford to live passively any longer. These people seem to have a plan for the child I am carrying. If I stay complacent, I'm afraid of what the child will be put through. I don't want them to have to live through what we did with Uncle Churchill. Just some pawns in the most disturbing game of chess.

My dear sister, I need to gather as much information as possible about what they could be planning. I've grown so anxious for this child and want to see if I can stop disaster before it strikes, and that is where I need your help. I need you to relay a message to Anthony since I can't reach him myself. Uncle Churchill has cut me off from all of you saying I now belong to my husband's family. That man makes my blood boil!

Anthony was always keen on listening in on what Uncle Churchill was up to. If there is anything that he knows that could be useful, please help me ask him to write me. I know he won't be able to write to me directly, but I ask that you pass his letters on to me. I'll find a way to get it from you.

I miss you all so much.

Nairo

Letter 2
Talika to Anthony
June 21, 1990

Dear Anthony,

I hope this finds you well. I wish I could say the same but I'm afraid it would be a lie. My heart is so heavy and my mind so unsettled. It took me days to finally start writing this letter to you. I know what became of our sister.

Uncle Churchill lied to us. Nairo is alive! She didn't run away from home neither is she dead somewhere in a ditch as he keeps saying. He married her off to one of his party members and then spun that story of her disappearance to cover his tracks. That wicked man has crossed a line I didn't even know existed!

The look of pain on your face since uncle told us that she was dead, has been burned into my mind, young brother. I'm glad that at least you can rest well knowing that our dear sister is alive.

Words cannot explain the joy I felt when I received a secret letter from Nairo. She had to send it to me at school and have it delivered to the administrator's office. I don't know how she managed to find my school or even get out of the house they keep her in.

111

Uncle has cut her off from any communication with us, and she is basically under lock and key.

I wish the joy I felt when I first began to read her letter lasted longer. As I read the contents my heart broke and tears began to run down my eyes. Not least because the sister I was told was dead had been sold off into marriage by our uncle for his political gain. I'll explain everything to you in greater detail when you come for visiting day this term. But things are not looking good.

I know you have been trying to get us to pay closer attention to Uncle Churchill's actions for years. You tried to get us to see that his wickedness was not something that could be ignored, but we turned a blind eye to both your words and his actions. Brother, you can't blame us for wanting nothing to do with it. Ignoring it was the only way we could get by and that's why Nairo always told us to hold our tongues. It was either Uncle Churchill or the cruel streets. We made our choice.

But we have reached a crossroads. We cannot sit back and watch this madman destroy our sister's life. It's even worse now that Nairo is with child. Anthony, that child is going to have to go through what we went through or much worse.

You, more than anyone, know the extent of Uncle Churchill's cruelty. Nairo has asked for your help. She needs to know everything that you know about what Uncle Churchill is plotting. She suspects that Uncle and that pig he married her off to have something horrible in store for her and her child, and I'm afraid she might be right. The problem is we don't know what that is. Please help Nairo and tell me everything you know. What could Uncle Churchill possibly stand to benefit from this marriage?

You know what to do with this letter.
Sincerely,
Talika.

Unraveled Threads

Letter 3
Anthony
to Talika

Dear Talika,

I'm overjoyed to hear that our sister is safe. But I can't say that it is good news. I think death would have been a better fate for our dear sister, for the man that she is now married to is worse than the devil himself.

Remember how I used to accompany Uncle Churchill to all his party rallies and listen in on his meetings? I must confess that at first, there was nothing more exciting to me than a group of men gathering together to fight for what they knew was right for the nation. These men were my heroes. Well dressed and outspoken, each one making more sense than the last. I believed they were the future of the nation.

They always spoke about what truly mattered to the people and fought to find solutions to the problems of the common man. I remember the fundraising events to build the hospital in our village so we didn't have to take the two-hour trip to the town. They worked tirelessly and brought real change to the community, not like the useless city politicians they always talked about. The ones whose only desire was to line their pockets and fill their bellies. The party took pride in never taking a dime for themselves. After all, it was the people's money. To steal from them would be to sell our nation's future.

As a child, these heroes gave me something to live for. Uncle Churchill once told me that his job was to fight corrupt and wicked people, the likes of which had killed our parents. To be one of the party members was to dedicate one's life to martyrdom. He told me that our father's death was not in vain and that his spirit would live on through those that continued to fight. These men were the heroes that we needed to free the people from the shackles of oppression. To me, they were the key to making sure that no one would ever have to go through what we went through. He has fed me this story for as long as I can remember.

Their ultimate goal, he told me, was to purge the nation of corruption by replacing corrupt leaders with good ones. It all made sense, right? Except they never seemed to want to stand for public office at any level and always let the publicly corrupt officials continue their operations, with the party controlling them from the shadows. They preferred to make puppets rather than replacements. When I asked why they let them stay in their cushy posts, I was told that holding political power was one of the fastest ways to grow corrupt and that 'only fools elect those that cannot make change where they stand.'

Now I know why I was put so close to Uncle Churchill. Actions I thought I was taking of my own accord were in truth Uncle Churchill's manipulation at work. I was being trained to be another one of his obedient puppets that would go on to gain him more power Unfortunately for him, the plan to radicalize me failed as soon as I saw this reality.

There is a lot that I have to tell you dear sister and in due time, all will be revealed, but, for now, I believe that the most important thing that both you and Nairo need to know is what became of our father and mother. Their deaths and the attempts to conceal the truth were the beginning of the end for the party.

I don't know much about our father. I have few memories of him and only know what you and Talika have told me about him. But one fact that is important for us to understand is that he was a good man. Yusuf and his twin brother, Nsia started The Golden Dragonfly Core, or as you and I know it, the GDC Party when they were fresh out of high school. You may not recognize these names, but these were the names given to our father and Uncle Churchill at birth. Yusuf was our father, and Churchill's real name is Nsia.

When Yusuf and Nsia were attending Dungu Senior Boys' Secondary School a few towns over from ours, they became very interested in the teachings of several socialist, Marxist, and communist authors. Learning about our nation's colonial history and seeing the vestiges of those systems around them, they began to see that they were indeed at the bottom of the food chain and that the way the nation was run would keep them and their people there unless they did something about it. They wanted to elevate the nation and give it the chance of joining the modern world and having an equal seat at the table.

One of their first acts was to change their names and adopt more Western names. To them, they had to first enter the halls of the elite and the upper echelons of society to gain the wealth and influence needed to make any mark. Yusuf chose to go by Raymond Maxwell after Karl Marx, a leader he greatly admired and one he saw as a misunderstood visionary. Nsia chose the name Matthew Churchill after the English prime minister that displayed a great love for his people and a tenacity to fight through all obstacles. A lot of the people around them thought that they had gone mad. But fueled by their misguided and idealistic dreams, they continued to preach their political gospel of virtue, compassion, and charity. The Golden Dragonfly Core grew to about fifty members in a very short time as they found favor in the eyes of the religious communities that espoused these same values. I don't have a detailed account of what happened during the next 12 years, but what I do know is that the three of us were born and Maxwell and Churchill gained some prominence in the political scene as the twin forces of justice, growing the party steadily until progress came to a halt after our fathers' death.

I've been able to piece together an account of how our father died from Uncle Churchill's version of the events, conversations I've had with former party members that left after Maxwell's death as well as Police documents that I got my hands on. Don't ask me how a 13-year-old managed to do this. I have my ways.

One day as our father and Uncle Churchill were walking home from their weekly meetings, Uncle Churchill suggested they take a shortcut through the eucalyptus forest near their houses since it was getting dark. Our father initially hesitated but eventually decided that it couldn't hurt to save some time. As they walked further down the narrow-forested footpath, Uncle Churchill said that the earth grew silent, as if warning of what was to come.

As they walked through the silent forest, surrounded by towering eucalyptus trees, they soon realized something. Though they knew their houses were not too far from where they were the clear footpath they had followed in had long faded and they were not sure where they were. Nevertheless, they marched on, guessing the general direction they should take. The sky began to darken as the sun set, and they knew that if they did not hurry, darkness would soon be upon them. As they continued to make their way in the vague direction of home, they heard rustling in the distance. Though it wasn't yet completely dark, the trees reduced their visibility and though they strained their eyes, they couldn't tell what it was.

Convinced it was probably a small animal and ignoring it, they pressed on. Suddenly three panga(machete)-wilding men with covered faces jumped out from the thicket and surrounded them. According to Uncle Churchill, they would not answer when asked what they wanted or who had sent them. The brothers knew that the chances of them making it out of that situation alive were slim. After about two minutes of trying in vain to get anything out of their assailants, the three men suddenly pounced forward at the two wielding their pangas high. Uncle Churchill quickly turned and run towards his house somehow navigating through the thick tree cover in the dim dusk. He knew that his house was probably about 200 meters away and ran for his life until he reached it, entered, and locked the door behind him. Just like today, he wasn't in the habit of locking his house when he went anywhere and this time, it saved his life.

Churchill never once looked back to see if his brother had followed him and in fear refused to even look out the window to see if his brother's house, which was just across from his, was open. He knew that Maxwell's three children, you me, and Nairo were at our grandmother's place with our mother at the time and was grateful he wouldn't have to risk his neck for us or be a hero at that moment. He spent the rest of the night hiding under his bed with a small knife in hand in case the assailants decided to invade his home.

The next morning, Uncle Churchill carefully looked out his window. There was no sign of the attackers! Not even a footprint in the mud. He looked for a sign that his brother had made it to his own house but found nothing that would suggest anyone other than him had been in the compound. He finally came out of his house at about noon and walked across the lawn to his brother's house. Churchill tried looking through the windows but the curtains were in the way so he listened closely for a bit but heard no signs of human life. Finally, he tried knocking on the door and there was no reply. The house was well and truly empty.

Shell-shocked, Churchill now had two options. He could either go back into the woods to look for his brother on his own: possibly stumbling upon the group that attacked him last night, or he could go to the GDC headquarters and tell the rest of the men what had happened in hopes that one of them had a better idea. Since he was certain there was a trap waiting for him if he went back through the woods, he decided to take the main road to the party headquarters, well away from the eucalyptus forest.

When later asked by the party members why he hadn't gone straight to the police, Churchill said that going to the police wasn't an option since the party was already greatly disliked by the local authorities. Besides, he would certainly be the top suspect.

Calling the GDC's main meeting place a headquarters was a stretch. In reality, it was a party member's living room. Churchill was certain they would all be there because he had scheduled a continuation of the previous day's meeting. When he got to the meeting winded and incoherent, he was met with questions as to why he was late and where his brother was. With terror in his eyes, Churchill recounted the events of the previous night to the group of men. After the initial shock and panic had calmed, they began to discuss what should be done about the matter. Again, going to the police wasn't an option since the party had made enemies of the authorities.

After much deliberation, they decided to form a search party of around thirty men to scout through the woods. Men both young and old spent the rest of the day carefully scanning every branch and twig for any clues as to what had happened, but they all found nothing. There was no evidence of a brutal attack or even a slight struggle. All that had been in that forest for the past decade were animals, insects, and plants. The group questioned Churchill, asking him to at least show them where they were attacked. He walked around the forest but couldn't point it out with certainty. One moment one branch would look familiar and the next it was like he'd never seen the forest before. He swore that they had indeed been attacked but couldn't provide any proof. The members of the search party asked why he hadn't called for help sooner and why he had left his brother behind, but he had no answers. He swore he was innocent and told the group that they need to focus on finding his brother's killers instead of accusing him.

No one had dared to suggest that Maxwell was dead and chastised Churchill for even mentioning it. They eventually concluded that he was most likely abducted and agreed to keep searching the next day. As the days went on and nothing more was found, one of the GDC members secretly went to the police. The police questioned every party member and took Churchill into custody for some time. But when their investigation turned up dry, they let him and the case was shelved.

Years went by but the attackers were never identified, and a body was never found. Several people were suspected to have been behind the attack, from members of rival political parties to GDC members that didn't agree with Maxwell's leadership style and even former lovers. At some point, our very own mother was a suspect. I remember when she came back from the station that day, distraught and heartbroken. She was never the same and we all know that is what eventually killed her. A lot of enemies were made during those years after Mother's death. The party members demanded that Uncle Churchill take care of us even though he was unwed. He reluctantly agreed and that's how we came to be with him.

In my opinion, none of the GDC members at the time were capable of such a thing as murder. They were all peace-loving, educated, simple men that had joined the party to fight the very thing they were accused of. I don't even have to defend our mother since we were with her at the time. And none of the rival political parties ever saw GDC as a serious rival since they vowed to never stand for public office. Maxwell was a man beloved by all except, of course, Churchill.

On the surface, Maxwell and Churchill's relationship appeared perfect: twin brothers that had been doing everything together since birth. They shared everything from clothes to ideologies and even built their houses on the same plot of land. They may have seemed well matched, but the truth is that Maxwell always shone a little brighter. Maxwell was the one that came up with the idea to start the Golden Dragonfly movement and though they acted as co- chairs, it was clear throughout its growth that Maxwell was the real boss. Churchill could never get any of his ideas, opinions, or plans past a conversation with Maxwell.

If Maxwell did not like it, it did not happen. What Churchill despised the most was the party's refusal to gain any real political power. At first, he went along with it, singing kumbaya with them all, but deep down he believed that without power, the party would fall into obsolescence. What change would they ever make if they never had any power?! The GDC's refusal to take any outright political action, going as far as refusing to vote made no sense to him. He saw his brother's insistence on absolute neutrality as a weakness and had spent years trying to convince his brother that they could never cause any real change unless they had power, money, and status but Maxwell never listened.

In the beginning, people bought into Maxwell's way of doing things. It was refreshing to see a leader that not only spoke of service but served. The GDC even became the most popular "political party" in the area. But as people saw how powerless they truly were, the support from the community began to wane. Though their numbers continued to grow, they did not translate into anything meaningful. They went from being a force for community change to solving petty squabbles between neighbors.

Churchill saw how his brother and the other members had deluded themselves into thinking they were doing something for the community when in fact, very little had ever come from their efforts. In his eyes, they were a joke and an embarrassment.

Of course, none of this was reason enough to kill his brother. But never the less, Uncle Churchill was the only one with anything close to a motive.

I can't tell you what to believe Talika. But based on the other things I've seen Uncle Churchill do, I'm very worried for Nairo. I'll tell you a lot more when I visit you in a few weeks. In the meantime, I will keep gathering information about this man that Nairo was married off to and see what more I can do on my end. Relay this information to Nairo, she needs to understand that when it comes to Churchill, always assumes the worst.

Please be safe.
Sincerely, Anthony.

Letter 4
From Talika To Nairo

Dear Nairo,

Words cannot express how glad I am to hear that you are safe. I cried for hours when Uncle Churchill told us of your disappearance. The thought of losing my only sister to some unknown fate was far too much to bare. Nevertheless, I had to keep up with my studies because I knew it is what you would have wanted for me. You always encouraged me to take books seriously but try as I may, my mind could think only of you. Something in my soul simply couldn't accept that you were gone. And here you are, alive and well. I pray for your continued health as well as that of your child every single day.

Though I was overjoyed to hear from you, the contents of your letter greatly unsettled me. To think that our Uncle could go as far as to sell you off for political gain is beyond anything I thought he was capable of. I hope that by the time you are reading this, you received the letter that I sent to you from Anthony detailing what happened to our father. I'm still in shock at learning about the truth behind his disappearance and even more frustrated at the fact that we have more questions now than answers.

I'm writing to let you know what Anthony and I discussed when he came to see me during my school's last visiting day. Learning about our father was shocking enough, but nothing could have prepared me for what he revealed next. I believe that Anthony and I have uncovered Uncle Churchill's true motive behind marrying you off to Charles and it's just as you feared, you and your child are in grave danger.

There are a lot of things you don't know about the man you now call your husband. His father grew up in our town and was close to both our father and Churchill. He was one of the first members of *The Golden Dragonfly Core* until he left for the city. The three of them agreed on most things except for one point that he would never compromise on. He aligned with most of the ideologies that the party stood for but did not like their desire to assimilate into Western culture, believing that a native-born system of governance should take priority. At some point, he left the GDC and moved to Kampala. We know that while in the city, he had a son, Charles. Charles's father became a wealthy and prominent businessman, using his money and connections to fund his political interests. One of his beneficiaries is the current member of parliament for our constituency. Charles himself has expressed interest in running for the seat in the past but never did for some unknown reason. I suspect Charles moved here to keep an eye on his father's political "investments." Perhaps his desire to stand was a clever excuse to get him here. When Uncle Churchill learned that the son of his former friend was coming back to our town, he invited Charles to join the GDC. The party has always been against standing for public office, but Uncle Churchill has been working hard to change that in the years after our father's death, and a wealthy partner like Charles's father would prove to be of great help. Charles was reluctant at first, weary of a man his father had chosen to part ways with but was eventually swayed by Uncle Churchill's gospel and agreed to join the GDC. To further solidify Charles's place in the party, Uncle Churchill managed to convince 70% of the party members to back Charles in the next election as their first-ever candidate for public office. This vote was later repealed when Charles himself announced that he would not stand but would prefer to help in the administration of the party, a move that infuriated Uncle, Churchill.

Uncle Churchill has never given up on his

dreams of becoming a political bigshot even after nearly 30 years and was not about to lose the benefits Charles brought. Making him the sole candidate of the party had failed so Uncle Churchill came up with a new plan. He knew that his long-time friend was a hopeless traditionalist who believed in strong family bonds. That's one of the only things we know for sure about Charles's mysterious father. What better way for Churchill to solidify his bond with his old friend than through marriage? Uncle Churchill married you off to Charles so he could be a part of a family with an extensive political network and vast wealth.

At first, I asked myself why Uncle Churchill didn't just run for MP himself or sign some sort of agreement with his friend directly if he wanted political power that badly. But Anthony quoted Uncle saying, *"Why waste time playing in the pond with small fish when you can wield the fishing rod? Or better yet, buy the pond!"* Uncle Churchill knows that the people with the real power don't sit in the rows of Parliament. The real power is held by those the MPs owe. If only he can control the nation's "leaders" then he can control the nation. He had learned this from watching Charles' father and that's why he wanted so badly to join their family. He knew that as a small- time charity, the GDC wouldn't be taken seriously, but if Charles's father would not invest in the GDC, he would certainly invest in his son.

Uncle Churchill plans to make Charles one of

his puppets and influence his father through him, con- trolling every decision that he makes from the shadows. As for your father-in-law, he re-sparked his new- found connection with Churchill, hoping he can be a good and upright influence on his son.

Uncle Churchill and Charles's father are planning something big. We don't know what exactly it is so we are helpless right now so all we can do is watch from the shadows. Nevertheless, I urge you to be cautious. We've seen what happens to those caught in Uncle Churchill's crosshairs. If there is any way you can get away from Charles and Uncle Churchill, then do so. I doubt they will let you go back to the village, but staying with Charles and his father might be more dangerous.

Truly Yours,
Talika

Wet Wings

I had no words. It was 3:00 a.m., and I had just spent the past two hours reading the letters I had found in the envelope, hoping with every passing sentence that I would get closer to some answers.
The tale that unraveled before me only got more and more sinister the further I read.

I slid back and lay on the floor of my room, staring at the ceiling for a while. My eyes followed the cracks that had formed over the years, and I wondered how deep they went. Were they only on the surface or just a chip away from bringing the whole building down? I tried in vain to collect my thoughts and come up with a plan of action that made sense. If what I read from these letters was true, then I couldn't handle this in the usual Jaliya way. I turned my head to the envelope and the very incriminating letters on the floor next to me and took a deep breath, dragging my palms down my face

"Why, of all people, did this have to happen to Jaliya!!!?"

Then I noticed something out of the corner of my eye. It was a small, blue, square piece of paper, a sticky note I think. It must have flown out of the envelope when I dumped everything out in panicked excitement. I reached down under the bed and picked it up. I don't know how I hadn't seen it earlier; I wasn't that far underneath.

On the note were three sentences scribbled in an adult's atrocious handwriting.

"Talika and her brother might pose more of a problem than we thought. Nairo's death will cause us more problems than we thought. I'm handling the situation but be ready to take action."

*"Okaaaaay. So, these two **are** murderers!!!"*

I stared at the envelope once more as the realization that this was evidence of several crimes on one tiny piece of paper. I placed the sticky note back into the folders with all the other letters and sat holding it in my hands.

"What am I supposed to do with this?"

I wasn't stupid. I knew the implications of this letter. Nairo was my father's first wife and something terrible must have happened to her and possibly her child. What I couldn't understand is why my mother married him! If she knew how terrible he and his fa- ther were, how could she do such a thing? And then there was my father. I knew he was an unfeeling man, but to go as far as to murder his wife, that, I couldn't believe. How had this injustice gone unsolved for 30 years?! Surely the police could have handled it. There

seems to be more than enough evidence in the world. Then again, Anthony said in that letter that the police never found anything.

"If things were that simple then they probably would have handled it a long time ago. These letters are enough to at least warrant an investigation. If they have been successfully hidden for 30 years then this is no simple matter.... this is only the beginning."

As I lay there, mind racing, my mind suddenly flashed back to the speech that Anthony had given. To the picture that he had held up and to the tears in his eyes. He knew who I was, there was no doubt about that. Otherwise, why would a grown man well into his 40s disguise himself as a high school student? And the name, *The Golden Dragonflies*; I can't believe I hadn't realized it sooner.

"The black card!"

I gasped, shooting off the floor. I opened my bedside drawer and sure enough, there it was, mixed with the mess of crumpled papers, rubber bands, and long-forgotten pencils. I picked it. The dragonfly sym- bol was the same as the one on the envelope! I had never dared to unfold it, too afraid to get involved in anything I could find no way out of. Turns out, I was already in the middle of something much worse than my overactive imagination could have conjured up. Whatever was written on this card must have been pretty important for Anthony to risk his neck to get it to me. He wanted me to find something and now, he owed me some answers.

I unfolded the card and on the inside was a phone number and nothing more. How anticlimactic. I honestly don't know what I expected but I sighed knowing that I was about to cross a point of no return. I dialed the phone number and it began to ring.

Riiiiiiing, riiiiiiing, riiiiiing.

"The number you have dialed is not available at the moment. Please try again later." Of course, it's not available, it's 3:00 a.m. on a Wednesday.

On the one hand, I was a bit disappointed. But on the other hand, I wave of relief washed over me. At least I didn't have to deal with this right now.

"He will see the missed call," I resolved as I dragged myself off the floor. My bones ached like I had been laying on concrete for hours...because I had been laying on concrete

for hours. I was surprised by how calm and reasonably I was acting. Everything in me should have been panicking and freaking up. Whatever the reason, it was probably for the best if I acted like nothing was wrong. As I said earlier, I couldn't handle this in the usual Jaliya way and need- ed to fight the burning desire to go screaming at my father and throw these letters in his face. Instead, I crawled under my covers and try and get some sleep. But even then, the undercurrents that would drown us all had begun to flow.

When I woke up at 5:00 a.m., aching bones exactly where I left them, it dawned on me that it would be a good idea to return the envelopes to my father's desk. By the looks of it, they had sat undisturbed in the drawer for a while, so I doubted he would check it immediately. But even if I wanted to return them, the key to the drawer was back in my parent's room, and there was no way I was risking sneaking back in at that hour.

As I was still trying to figure out what to do with the damn envelope, my phone began to ring. My heart sank straight to the center of the earth. I reluctantly answered the phone and heard the familiar voice of a man at the other end of the call.

"Jaliya, I thought you would never call."

PART THREE

"The tongue cannot claim to be ignorant of
what the teeth are doing."
-African Proverb-

***

The Madness of Hope

"That's no way to greet your uncle!"

This tall, thin, dark-skinned fellow I had once known as Tony, my classmate and club leader, was now introducing himself like he hadn't just committed identity fraud! I mean, I did know him as Anthony. But he wasn't the Anthony he claimed to be. He stood in the doorway of a one-room rental apartment in a pretty sketchy area on the outskirts of the city with a stupid grin on his face that made me want to punch him. Was he not going to take any of this seriously?!

It was a miracle I had even made it there in the first place. I hadn't slept a wink after 5:00 am when I initially woke up. Despite my best efforts, the contents of the letters stayed afloat in my head, replaying over and over hoping that something would help me make sense of things. Then there was the matter of returning the damn envelope to my father's study! After I received his call, Anthony had given me an address and said to meet him there at 1:00 p.m. exactly.

"Don't be late," were the last words I heard before he rudely hung up the phone.

Later that morning, I managed to convince my parents that I was going to do a bit of shopping in town. I don't know if they were catching on to my lies or if I was growing paranoid, but I just knew they were not buying it. Either way, there was no direct opposition to my plans.

I took a boda boda straight to the address Anthony had given me and ended up in front of a rusty black gate. It was one of those compounds with a cluster of one-room rental units that were common in the suburbs surrounding the capital. There was a small shop built into one of the walls and I stopped there to grab a soda and some small cakes to make up for the missed breakfast. I was too nervous and nauseous to eat but I didn't want to collapse at a time like this. It's funny how the nerves that had kept me from my meal were now making the hunger they had caused more excruciating than it needed to be. I stuffed the goods into my backpack and then stepped into the already open gate door. Anthony had told me exactly which door to knock on and so I did. Knock knock knock knock.

After a few moments, I heard some rustling and incoherent mumbling from inside the room. Then the curtain on the front window moved slightly and from behind it, one-half of a very wide-eyed face emerged. As quickly as it appeared, it disappeared, drew the curtain, and began to unlock an unreasonable number of padlocks. One after the other, they clicked and clanked until, finally, the door screeched open.

"Aren't you going to greet your uncle?" he said with the classic Anthony grin as he leaned against the door frame. The entire way there I had wondered if I should treat him as a former classmate and peer or with the respect deserving of an uncle. But his childish and obnoxiously unserious manner immediately settled it. Anthony and Tony truly were the same.

Laughing, I said, *"Aren't you going to invite your niece inside first?"*
With a mock bow, he gestured for me to step inside.

"Well then come in."
He was older than he looked but acted no different from all the other boys my age. I squinted my eyes as they adjusted to the dimly lit room. There was nothing in the room but a small wooden bench, a single plastic chair, and a bunch of papers scattered across the floor. On top of the mysterious stains on the wall and a foul smell I couldn't place, an occasional cockroach scurried across the floor. I jumped and covered my nose as the pungent odor and bug sighting caught me off guard.

"Please don't tell me this is where you stay."

Not only did he act like an adolescent, but he also lived like an unsupervised 12-year-old!

He burst into a bout of hysterical laughter. *"You act just like your father. He he. Of course, I don't live here. "This is my office, or maybe 'hideout' is a better word. There is no way I would stay in such an easy-to-locate place. Not with Churchill hot on my tail."*

My eyes grew wide when he mentioned Churchill's name. Seeing this change in expression, he suddenly got very, very serious. He placed his hand on my shoulder and gestured for me to sit down on the bench.

"Take a seat Jaliya; we have a lot to talk about."

I sighed at the sight of the splinter-filled bench in the corner. I would have never sat on such a structurally unsound piece of furniture but that comment about me being like my father rubbed me the wrong way. I reluctantly placed my backpack on the bench and sat next to it in an attempt to prove that I wasn't that prude.

"Did you bring the envelope you told me about?" He asked.

"Yes, I did." I replied reaching for my bag. When we spoke the night before, I had told him about the letters and notes, and he asked me to bring them along with me. I had told him that it was risky and that I wanted to return them, but

he insisted that I bring them, saying he should at least make copies before I returned them.

As I unzipped my bag to get the envelope out, I questioned why I had ever agreed to this. Anthony fell into the single plastic chair in the middle of the room and leaned forward in anticipation placing his elbows on his knees. Staring intently at the pile of newspapers, cut-outs, and photographs on the floor, his eyes began to dart back and forth like a hawk searching for a mouse in the thicket.

"Here they are," I said, stretching my hand out with the envelope. Without looking at me, he reached out for the envelope and opened it in one smooth motion. Rude! We sat in silence for about fifteen minutes as he read through the letters one by one, his eyes darting rapidly across them. When had finally read the last of the letters he broke the silence.

"Where are the rest of them Jaliya?"

Confused I asked, *"The rest of what?"*

"The rest of the letters. There are only four here. My sisters and I sent dozens of letters back and forth. I thought you had all of them."

"I don't know about any other letters. These are the ones that I found in my father's study yesterday." "Are you sure about that? You might have

missed some or dropped them."

"I swear these are the only letters that I found. I searched every inch of that study and this is all that came up."

Visiblyfrustrated,healmostthrewthe envelope to the wall but stopped before it went flying out of his hands. I was like someone had hit the pause button. His gaze then softened and his hands lowered. *"Why am I so surprised? Uncle Churchill probably destroyed them a long time ago. These were probably sent to your grandfather to emphasize the gravity of the situation."*

Turning to look at me, the grim scowl on his face disappeared in half a second. He was back to his bright charismatic self, eyes widening with each syllable.

"No! He must have destroyed the other letters and kept the least incriminating of them all to blackmail Charles. There is no way Uncle Churchill would give them to him unless he was using them as a threat. He knows what it would mean if these letters were found there. It may seem like a stupid move but that slick hyena knows how to back someone into a corner. The question is why?"

The sudden change in temperament caught me off-guard, but his words unfortunately made sense. If Uncle Churchill's goal was to use my father as a puppet, then threats wouldn't be off the table as a means of control. He probably sent them when my father and mother had tried to cut ties with him. Though it made sense, I wondered how the letters had come into Churchill's possession in the first place.

"How many letters were there originally? And why didn't you destroy them like your sister had asked you to do in the first place?"

He got up from his seat and crouched down on the floor, carefully flipping through the mess of papers as he replied.

"Because I was compiling evidence."

"I don't get it. He could always destroy the letters if he found them or play them off as the paranoid delusions of three traumatized kids. How could this possibly be evidence against him?"

He sighed and looked up at me annoyed and growing impatient.

"You're right. It would be dumb for me to keep the letters as evidence against Uncle Churchill. So, it's a good thing that's not what this is evidence of."

He pulled out what looked like a newspaper from years ago and handed it to me. It smelled of dust, cobwebs, and mildew and had had its fair share of rats come across it.

"This looks like it's a hundred years old!"

"If this were a hundred years old then I would be a fossil."

He pointed at the date and continued, *"This was an article released two years after my father's disappearance. Read what it says in the bottom right paragraph."*

There were three columns on the front page. The one in the center was the widest and had the headline, which was something about Richard Nixon's resignation, and underneath it a smaller headline on a bill being passed by Parliament. The two columns to either side were thinner, and then the one to the left was the breakdown of the country's economic status. The rest of the left column was advertisements. The column to the right was the thinnest – and there it was in faded print.

"UNIDENTIFIED MAN FOUND DEAD IN FOREST!"

As I read this, my eyes widened and my hands grew cold. Then Anthony's sharp voice cut through the silence,

"Who do you suspect that 'local man' was?"

He spoke as if he wasn't sure. How could he not have known? Just a moment ago, I thought I was holding an article on my grandfather's murder, but his unsure tone brought me to question that.

"You mean you don't know?" I asked. I was already emotionally drained and had come here looking for some clarity. So, I did not

appreciate the roller-coaster this interaction was proving to be.

Looking at me like I was missing something extremely obvious.

"What didn't you get about UNIDENTIFIED? When they found that body, the animals had long gotten to it. It was nothing but a few bones and scraps of cloth."

"So, this might not have even been Maxwell,"

I said to myself, half disappointed but also relieved.

"Do you always refer to your grandfather by his first name?" Anthony asked with a chuckle.

"I didn't even know about this grandfather until last night." I huffed.

"You could at least use his real name," he said, continuing to vex me. I had to remind myself that despite his behavior, this man-child was still my uncle.

"Can you please just tell me if this was him or not?"

"I can't do that because I don't know. The GDC members say they never saw any trace of a struggle. When that body was found, almost every bone was broken, and whoever it was had been dead for approximately three years. Though most of the clothes were ruined, they did find one thing still intact – a Golden Dragonfly pin. Everyone that was in the know automatically thought that was

the end of the matter. By then it had become the popular symbol of the GDC. That wasn't the case three years prior when the man was said to have died."

"So, either this person died much later one or....did someone go back to the body after it had long been dead and planted the pin?" I asked, struggling to wrap my head around his words.

"Sharp girl. It's one of those two. I personally think it was planted there. The only person that had one of those pins at the time the man is said to have died, was my father. You'd think that would point to it being his body, right? Here is the thing though, a few days before his disappearance, he had given it to me when he left us with our grandmother and mother."

"so you had the pin when he disappeared?" "Yes, I did. I don't know whether that body was my father's or not. What I do know is that someone wanted everyone to believe that it was."

"Urgh. This is hurting my brain. What kind of messed up psychos would do that?"

"There are a lot of messed up psychos in this world Jaliya. You can always count on that."

I sat in silent thought for a few minutes. Turning the situation over in my head. It had been so many years and still not one person had the answer. If I couldn't know that mystery, I can at least have my crazy uncle answer a few of my other questions.

"Anthony, one thing I don't understand, among many, many, many things, is why they went as far as changing their names. Maxwell and Churchill I mean. It doesn't sit right with me. I know you said in the letter that was to assimilate into a certain culture, but at this point, I'm assuming everything has a deeper and more sinister reason. Was that also a deliberate plan or part of your conspiracy?"

He looked a bit surprised at my question but began to speak as he crouched back down to the pile of papers on the floor.

"That was Churchill's idea."

He picked out some photos from the mess and shuffled them in his hands. And continued,

"If you ask me, which you just did, I think he was preparing for his future in politics. I'm sure your woke alarm is going off right now, but you have to apply context to every situation Jaliya. Today, you and I call such people thoroughly colonized, but back then, those were the educated. It was certainly deliberate, but they were hardly the only ones to do it. That might be the one thing that isn't that deep."

"That makes some sense I suppose," I said, satisfied with his answer.

"Come here and look at these photos." He laid about five photos in a line on the floor. I got up from the bench and sat on the floor next

to him. Handing me the first one, he said, *"This was Nairo and Charles on their wedding day."*

I saw my mother standing in her simple, lace, A-line gown, with no light in her eyes.

"So, this is what my mother looked like on what was supposed to be the happiest day of her life."

Charles smirked at that statement.

"I think you'd look the same way if you were being forced into a marriage."

I picked up the second photo, the same photo he had shown me and the other club members on the last day of school.

"You gave quite the performance that day. Do you know how many sleepless nights that speech brought me?" I said, half joking.

Anthony laughed and picking the picture out of my hand, said,

"I was counting on it."

"What is that supposed to mean?" I asked, my curiosity peaking.

"I didn't disguise myself as a teenager and join that school of yours just to play dress up. I *was on a mission."*

"oh really? I'm guessing I was that mission," I said, again, half joking.

"Well, partially. My original goal was to get through to Talika since she had completely cut me off. But things got.... let's say they got complicated along the way.

I realized that I had to get you to somehow do the digging for me. Hence my little performance. I was counting on you being like your mother, and I was right. Pulling at your heartstrings got the job done."

"That's straight-up manipulation," I said a little repulsed by his tactics.

He leaned back onto his hands and replied, *"Well, I've learned from the best."*

What did he mean by that? Up until then, I had brushed his emotional flip-flopping off, but after that statement, it began to bother me a lot more. I guess this concern showed on my face because he laughed and answered my unspoken question.

"Oh, come on. Did it never occur to you that a man that snuck into a secondary school and disguised himself as a teenager was trouble? It seems Talika failed to teach you the concept of stranger danger."

"..........Why aren't you and my mother on speaking terms?" I asked him. That pause wasn't intentional; it was just that I had not yet processed that side of this whole situation.

"Talika and I aren't on speaking terms because she is a coward. After Nairo's death, she grew weak and decided to play it safe."

"I'm guessing marrying my father was the safest bet?"

"At the time it was. Nairo's death was another cloud hanging over Churchill's head and he needed a way to cover his tracks. Since Nairo had never really been seen in public as Charles's wife, it was a lot easier to simply replace her."

"So, you're telling me that my mother.... has been acting as Nairo all this time?"

"Yes. That is exactly what I am saying." My shoulders slumped as all the life drained out of me.

The thought that this woman I had been calling my mother all this time was meant to be a replacement for her dead sister. Was life that cheap to these people?

"Do you know what happened to Nairo?" I asked almost in a whisper. For a moment, he looked at me with pity in his eyes, an expression I had never seen on his face, but it quickly faded back to apathy.

"I've spent the past twenty years trying to find out. But Churchill is great at cleaning up his tracks. When Talika agreed to replace Nairo, I was cut off from her just like we were cut off from Nairo. Churchill warned me not to try and get in contact with her or it would be the end of me. Being the idiot I was, I tried to get in contact with her anyway. Just like you, I needed answers. Unfortunately, Churchill always keeps his promises. I was shunned by the entire GDC and was kicked out of the university that Uncle Churchill had been paying for. Homeless and

alone, I almost ran mad with grief. There was only one place I could turn."

I looked up at him with anticipation as he continued. Hoping and praying that there was one good person in this saga. But my heart dropped at his answer.

" Churchill himself."

"WHAT! You went to that monster for help! Didn't you just describe how he ruined your life?!"

I couldn't make sense of it. Who goes back to a family that disowned them. As I looked down at him hovering over his pile of papers, this uncle of mine looked less like the fountain of answers I was looking for and more like a bumbling conspiracy theorist in way over his head!

"I'm not here to win any Nobel prizes Jaliya. He said almost as if he had read my mind. *"It was either that or death,"*

"Then you die!"

His attempt to justify any of this did not impress me one bit. My repugnance caught him a little off-guard, but he chuckled instead.

"You of all people should be grateful that I chose life. How would I avenge her death if I too was dead oh righteous one? Is it not you that wants justice? Or am I wrong? As messed up as it sounds, Churchill was the closest thing to a

family I had ever had. Even Talika and Nairo had looked at me as insane for most of my life. They only ever listened to me when...."

He paused for a second as the resentment he had been hiding for years began to show its ugly face.

"That's irrelevant now. When I went to Churchill, I was like a wrenched dog, starving, abandoned, and broken. Luckily for me, Churchill has some use for such wretched dogs. I had always paid close attention to GDC matters and my insight proved useful to him. He made me a sort of spy in the party and would send me to the different Golden Dragonfly centers to spy on his 'chickens', as he called them."

"You still sound like a complete sell-out to me!"

I was no longer hiding my feelings on the matter and the disdain showed on my face. He let out a sigh, his face growing more solemn before he continued.

"There was no day that went by without me thinking of my sisters, and more importantly, how I could take Churchill down. I spent years trying to find something to get him with, but as I said, Churchill keeps things clean. Eventually, I realized that my only hope was Talika. But trying to get through to her was not going to be easy. Though Churchill and I were buddies again, I was still banned from all forms of contact with Talika. The only hope I had was to get her to

contact me. Then I began my plan. I found out that Nairo's daughter went to a certain high school. If there was even the slightest risk to her, I knew Talika would react. I somehow convinced Churchill that the best way to increase our support for the next elections was to get the youth on our side. I suggested we target secondary schools and set up clubs that pushed our agenda. By the time the next elections rolled around, they would be an invaluable resource for the Party. I even managed to convince him that I should go and set one of them up myself as a prototype to prove to him how great of an idea this was. I had my bait in hand. It was a matter of throwing it into the lake, and the fish were bound to come."

"Was dressing up like a teenager part of your original plan?"
This all sounded so ridiculous to me and I couldn't help but mock him.
"Not initially, but the school wasn't too keen on letting an outsider in for the sole purpose of political indoctrination. A good school I must say, but that was very bad for me. With Churchill breathing down my neck, I changed tactics. Disguising myself as a student was the only choice I had. That way I could get Churchill's work done as well as fulfill my original goal. Unfortunately for me, the fish did not bite. Talika was too careful and

refused to show her face. So, you were my last hope. I had to convince Talika that Nairo's precious child was going down the path she had tried so hard to protect her from."

"Did it work?" Finally, I was getting some answers.

"A little too well. Talika ratted me out to Churchill when you began acting strange and I had to make a run for it. But Talika never contacted me herself. Luckily for me, another fish fell for my bait, hook, line, and sinker."

I knew exactly what he meant and I wasn't too pleased about being dragged into this.

"So Nairo's child somehow survived and happened to go to the same school as your other sister's daughter."

I hadn't questioned it up until then, but something wasn't adding up. I had assumed that the child Nairo birthed was dead or was never even born. Anthony stood up, walked over to his dingy plastic chair, and sat down, leaning back and waving his hands dramatically as he spoke.

"What do you think happened to Nairo's unborn child Jaliya?"

I went silent. Didn't she just tell me she somehow survived and was going to my school? Maybe she was in Churchill's care or something. How was I supposed to know?

"Oh my god Jaliya, I thought you were smarter than that. YOU ARE NAIRO'S CHILD!"

".w.wh...wha...what... how?"

"She gave birth to you a few months before she disappeared. Talika raised you all these years as her own just as Uncle Churchill had instructed her. Honestly, how could you not have seen it?!"

I stood there in silence trying my best to fight the tears that wanted to drown my face. I wanted so desperately to say something to this cruel man. To tell him that he was wrong. To argue. To fight. To say Anything!! But all I could do was stand there, choking on every word that tried to make its way out.

"Wow, that was hard to watch," he said mockingly. "It was pretty obvious from the start. But I can't blame you too much. Churchill and your father watch both you and her like hawks. Even if she wanted to tell you, she couldn't. I know her intention was never to lie to you. Luckily I was eventually able to get through to her through a mutual contact."

"What mutual contact?" Gritting my teeth, I finally asked. My ears were ringing but now I had to know everything. Who else was a part of this web of lies?

"Calm down vindicator. It's no one you know. One of the GDC members from our hometown managed to keep in touch with both of us over the years. Somehow Churchill had

missed this connection and I was able to receive a message from Talika through him."

"I'm guessing this was another secret letter." "You're right. It was another letter. But this

time it was coded."

"What did the letter say?"

In a flat and expressionless tone, he said, *" Something along the lines of 'Leave my daughter out of this and stay away from us you traitor'."*

"Where is it? Can I see it?"

"No," he replied in that same flat tone.

"Why? Is it fair to hide it from me at this point? You've been brutal with your revelations up until now. So why hide anything."

He replied once more in that calm and even tone. *"I burned it."*

"Why would you do that?"

"If I hadn't done that, Churchill would have found it and all four of us would be in for it."

I sat on the floor for a while in silence, perhaps hoping that he would say something more, but he didn't. He crouched down in his seat and began to flip through the papers on the floor in front of me. After a few minutes of stunned silence, I finally spoke.

"So, what now?"

"I'm sorry?"

I stood up and repeated myself.

"What now? You just told me that my entire life is not only a lie but a hopeless web of lies! I can't just go back to living my normal life. Not when I know my 'mom' is my dead mother's sister. Not when the mother and grandfather I have just learned of were probably murdered. Not when I know that my father and Churchill are probably behind these murders. Oh, God. And then there is my father. Whose side is he on? What part of this twisted game is he playing? All this coming to light because my crazy uncle dressed up as a teenager to infiltrate my school under the guise of setting up a political indoctrination unit? What the hell am I supposed to do with all this?! You told me all this for a reason, right!"

I paced around the room, every word hitting me like a brick one after the other. I looked at him desperate for the smallest hint of hope. I simply couldn't leave things the way that they were now.

"Should we call the police? You said you were collecting evidence, right? Is this even solid evidence of anything? Do we try to find out? Oh, God! It will probably only get worse from here. What Now!"

All the while I talked, Anthony had sat comfortably in his chair. He leaned back and looked at me with a distant stare.

"I ask myself the same question every day Jaliya. And I would be lying if I told you that I knew. The secrets of the Golden Dragonfly run deeper than even I could have imagined. As for why I told you, you needed to know the truth. These people use those that don't know who they are. If I didn't tell you...."

"You don't know. So, you went against the most dangerous people you know of, dug up dirt and now that you've found skeletons, you say you don't know? And as for that nonsense of telling me the truth for my own sake, I don't buy I....."

Anthony stood up and cut me off and spoke with a massive, deranged grin. *"Yes, you pretty much summed it up Jaliya. I don't know. But don't judge me too harshly. You and I are one and the same. We both just can't resist a good mystery."*

I couldn't believe what I was hearing! This man was a clown!

"OH, MY GOD! Can you hear yourself talk?

You sound like a madman."

After a brief moment of once more questioning everything about my life, I took a deep breath, walked to the bench, and sat down, burying my head in my palms.

"Anthony, why did you drag me into this mess? Sure, this all affects me and it's not like I have nothing to do with it. But was leaving me clueless not an option? Was it really necessary to

give me this impossible weight to bear? If there really is nothing we can do, then why put me through all this? What was your goal here?"

He walked over to the bench and sat next to me.

"I know how you feel right now Jaliya. When my sisters first sent me those letters, I felt like I was being dragged into something I had tried so hard to stay away from. I was perfectly content watching Uncle Churchill from within the organization, hoping that if he ever tried anything, I would be able to protect my sisters. I learned early on that Uncle Churchill was a bad man. Even at eight years old, I could see it. But I couldn't fight him. I had hoped my father would be able to protect us, but when he died we had to survive. My survival strategy has always been to stay informed, stay close, and stay on Uncle Churchill's good side. But I have never deluded myself into thinking that he cares about anyone. I knew I was only one wrong move away from disappearing as well. That has been my reality since I was a child and over 30 years later, it's still the case."

"At least you had some knowledge to help you navigate that minefield. I have been completely unaware of this until now. I could always feel the undercurrents in my father's life. But I always chalked it up to his work....whatever that was. I knew enough to stay as far away from it as possible and they both encouraged this."

"Well, here is the thing. I didn't exactly know how to tell you this and have been debating if I should for a long time. I know you don't want to hear any of this, especially about your parents. But you came here for the truth, and I can't let you leave without it."

"What are you saying? Please don't tell me there is more."

He ignored me and kept on talking.

"Talika has worked hard to keep you away from all of this, but your father's involvement with Churchill is more sinister than any of us know. You are not safe as long as you are with those two, no matter what you believe. You can't hope to stay secure from the lion in the lion's den. So I have to tell you more...."

As he spoke, something snapped within me.

"...stop. Just stop. I've heard enough."

I got up from the bench and began packing my things into my backpack.

*"What are you doing Jaliya?"*Anthony asked as I reached around the room for the letters I had brought and started placing them back into the envelope.

"What does it look like? I'm going home. If I'm lucky my father hasn't noticed this damn envelope is missing, and I can put it back where I found it and live my life like I never met you!"

"What life do you think you are going back to? Jaliya you can't just walk away from this. Sooner or later you are going to find

yourself entangled in an even worse mess. They are grooming you for something horrible. That's the only reason they didn't kill you with your mother."

I snapped back and stared straight into his eyes.

"Don't act like I have another choice."

He grabbed my shoulders and spoke as solemnly as before.

"Yes, you do. You always have a choice. And take it from me, running away is not the sustainable one. Once you know the truth it hunts you down like a jackal. You can't run from this."

"Oh yes, I can. I get my acting skills from you."

I zipped up my backpack, picked it up from the bench, and began for the door ready to escape that dark, dingy room and leave all this behind forever.

"Jaliya, listen to me. You can't go back. Whether it was from me or Churchill or your father or even Talika, you were bound to hear this all at some point. There is so much more you need to understand because where things are going, you as the only hope we have."

I stopped and turned to look at him, shivering with fear and anger. What on earth was this man expecting from me? And how dare he drag me into this mess and proceed to insinuate that I was the one to clean it up.

"Whose only hope, am I? How unfortunate they are because I am not signing up to be the third missing person! You and your sister can go to the Police and deal with this yourselves. I want nothing to do with any of this. Nothing!"

"No, we can't go to the police and you know that. The evidence we have is circumstantial at best. But, Jaliya, that is not the point. Churchill is onto us. Please listen to me."

"I thought you said that your mutual contact with Talika was watertight. What do you mean Churchill is onto you?"

The knot in my stomach began to grow and my heart beat faster and faster.

*"Not just me. **Us.** As I said, you can't leave now. Going back in there ignorant would be like walking into the lion's jaws. The difference between life and death is knowledge, and your ignorance will make you the perfect target for Churchill's manipulation. And about that contact, I never said they were watertight." "So, you think Churchill is planning to use me for something?"* I said getting even more anxious by the second.

"I'm certain of it. That contact I had suddenly dropped off the face of the earth after giving me the information I needed. When I got to my place this morning, it was a mess. I spent last night here reading through what I had collected over the years trying to piece together something to hook Churchill. Then you called and I told you to

meet me. I went to the place I've been staying to freshen up before you came but when I got there, the place had been turned upside down. Luckily, I had kept everything here and they hadn't discovered this place. But again, with Churchill, it's only a matter of time. He didn't want us to meet for a reason. Please use your head."

"What could they have been looking for? Does Churchill know that you're trying to sabotage him? You already told me you have nothing substantial. If he's watching you that closely he should know that. Why blatantly come after you now?"

"That's my point. The only reason Churchill has left me alone up until this point is that he knew I had nothing. Now that he has started showing his fangs, I know I must be close to something – or rather, someone."

He walked back to the pile of papers on the floor, sat down, and began filing through them as he spoke,

"In the message she sent, Talika warned that I needed to stay away from you. This wasn't her maternal instincts. She might have fooled Churchill by playing the role of a loving mother, but I know Talika too well. She is cold and calculating. What she was saying is that you, my dear niece, are a weapon Uncle Churchill was planning to start building. He knew very well that

*was **your** school. He has also been watching you and knows you're the kind of person to eat all that justice nonsense up. What he didn't count on was that either I or Talika would successfully send a message either way. Now that he knows I have access to you, he wants to know how much you know so he can make his next move. I was never supposed to find that mess at my place. If I hadn't switched up my schedule, I would never have known they were there."*

If Talika was working for Churchill and they somehow found out where I was, would I be safe if I went back home? I was shivering with fear at the very thought.

"Sss...ssoo, whose side is...Talika on?"

Anthony jumped up and threw a stack of papers he had been scanning through on the ground in frustration.

"I don't know! I can't figure her out. That's why I had to get to you and tell you all this."

He then looked back at me with an emotion I had never seen him display – fear.

"Listen Jaliya, I don't blame you for not knowing any of this. And I am genuinely sorry. But there is no time for childish stubbornness. You are in a very dangerous position and need to be very, very careful. God knows what will happen to you otherwise. Trust me, there are fates worse than death. I know what Churchill and Charles are capable of. The fact that you are Charles' child doesn't exempt you from their

rules. If they can erase Nairo and my father, imagine what fresh hell they will dream up for you. Family means nothing to them."

I stood there and stared at him unable to utter a single word. Then I felt the tears begin to flow. The fear and pain in his voice ripped whatever shroud of confidence I had in my safety. I was terrified.

"I.... I.... don't understand what you want from me. What....do you want me to do?" I asked in a whisper through my sobs.

When he saw the tears in my eyes, Anthony began to calm down. *"Jaliya, I get it, this is a lot. But I don't want to die. Neither do I want my sister or you to die. These men are cruel and weakness isn't something you can afford. We all have to come together to figure this out. I can't do this on my own. I need both you and Talika to help me."*

"How am I a threat to them? I'm just a dumb kid. You're the one who just had to open up this can of worms. Talika at least tried to avoid trouble until you came waltzing in here with your hero complex."

I wiped the tears from my face and looked up at him.

"Why should I believe anything you say anyway? You're either half-crazy or a hundred percent crazy. Why should I believe

the babblings of an emotionally unstable man-child? I don't know what
you have to gain by telling me these horrible things, but you have no concrete evidence to show me that Churchill and my father are such monsters. Sure, they are politicians, but you don't even have proof that they are murderers. I'm not going to naively eat up every word that you say."

Anthony looked at me in silence for a few seconds, as if in deep thought. The disappointment on his face could not be hidden. Then he spoke like the calm considerate adult he should have been acting like the entire time.

"You are right. I don't have any proof. And you have no reason to believe a word I say. And yes, I am crazy. I must have been crazy bringing a virtual child into this."

He took a deep breath and looked at the pile of papers on the floor.

"Just do me one favor. Keep all this to yourself. If you aren't going to help me solve this, then you can at least help me protect yourself and your mother. Act like nothing ever happened and if possible, drop off the face of the earth. Get away from them and hide until you get a message from me that the
coast is clear. I was not able to save your mother but hopefully, it's not too late for you."

He pulled up a small, folded piece of paper from his pocket and handed it to me.

"And for goodness sake, Jaliya, trust no one and especially not Mar..."

Before he could complete his sentence I stuffed the paper into my bag and ran out the door never once looking back.

When I got home I went straight to my room. Luckily for me, my father was out and Talika was in the garden tending to her rose bushes. I locked the door behind me, threw my bag into my closet, covered it with some clothes, and crawled under my covers. The next few days of my life dragged on and every minute was excruciating. I thought about what Anthony had said and made my decision. If there was even the slightest possibility that he was right, taking his advice was my best bet. My parents might not have been who or what they said they were, but I still loved them. They had worked to keep me out of this mess for as long as possible so the least I could do for all three of us was remove myself from the picture. But until I could figure that out, I needed to act like nothing ever happened. And so, life went on as normal.

One morning we were watching the news at breakfast a few weeks after I had met with Anthony, and a breaking news story came onto the television. It was a video clip of a man in a black and gold suit jumping off a 6-story building to his death. They were able to identify who the man was from the ID and business cards in his pocket. The name on the cards was Robert Anthony Churchill. I froze as I realized who it was.

In The Sun

A cold, hard wind blew across the land that day as grey clouds threatened to drench us all. It was the second time I had been to the little town my mother had grown up in and just like last time, it was for a funeral. The only difference was that this time, I was old enough to know what was going on.

Only two days after we had watched Anthony jump on live television, I was staring at a polished mahogany casket that held whatever remained of him, on a stand at the pulpit. It was a closed casket ceremony to save the mourners from a gruesome sight. The small chapel was full of family members, a few I had met over the years, but most I had never met. They all seemed sad but none more than Talika, my stepmother. The rest of them sat solemn and sad but did not seem too shocked about his death. It was as if this was something they had been expecting. After the brief funeral service, the close family members proceeded to the grounds that would be Anthony's final resting place.

The fact that I had seen him only weeks before was all I could think about. My feelings were complicated by the awful circumstances around our meeting. I had wondered how my parents were going to explain the situation to me. But they told me that Anthony was my mother's estranged brother whom she hadn't spoken to for years. I was angry at their manipulation of the situation. The least they could have done was tell me why they say he was estranged rather than give me such a lame excuse. It was lazy. At the very least what they told me was partially true. I mourned for him in his capacity as a friend, and uncle, and the only one that dared to tell me the truth. Unfortunately, he had taken most of the secrets he had tried to tell me to his grave and since I had chosen to walk away, I would probably never know. I replayed his words over and over in my head.

"your *ignorance will make you the perfect target ....*"

What if the burden of all the things he knew was too heavy for him to bear on his own? Would he go as far as to take his own life? He had said that Churchill was on his tail. As unhinged as he was, I had only seen a flash of fear in his eyes once. This was a man that has spent his life chasing the truth. Had he given up? Even though he had given up, I couldn't believe that his death was an accident or a suicide as it appeared. There had to be something more to this.

My thoughts went to the crumpled-up letter that sat in my backpack at home and I couldn't help but wonder if giving Talika that letter could have changed anything. I had completely ignored it and chosen not to give it to her. How would that have looked? The millions of questions she would ask and my lack of answers would certainly lead us down a dangerous path. I couldn't take that risk. Sure, there was probably a non-suspicious way to give it to her. But I didn't want any of this to trace back to me. Did I do the right thing?

The drive home that evening was as solemn as the day had been. My father drove in silence as my stepmom and I sat in the back. She was inconsolable the entire time and I had to keep calming her down whilst also stopping my own emotions from bubbling over. Acting like I knew nothing of what was going on was proving to be harder than I thought. My father was silent for most of the ride, but when he did speak, he made some sterile comments about how unfortunate this all was.

I had grown very suspicious of my father since my meeting with Anthony and paid close attention to how or what he spoke. I wanted to remain respectful because I had no proof of anything Anthony said, but his calm and callous manner about this terrified me. I couldn't help but wonder if he had something to do with Anthony's death. Would what happened to Anthony happen to me if I had stayed and listened to all he had to say? Anthony said that ignorance was deadly but it looked to me like knowing too much was far worse. As I wrestled with these thoughts, another thought slowly began to worm its way in. Would Anthony still be alive if I had stayed and listened to him? Was it my fault he was dead? This thought turned from a whisper to a blaring horn as tears ran down my face and for once, I didn't fight them. I felt I had no right to shed any since I had abandoned him.

When we got home, I helped my stepmother to her room and then made my way to my own. I took a long warm shower to try and ease the stiffness I felt in my joints. I was tired, hungry, and beyond my breaking point. As the warm water rolled down my back, the tears began to flow once more. This time it wasn't only about Anthony's death; it was everything. I now had to bear the weight of all I knew alone. Even though I had chosen to walk away, at least I knew that there was someone dedicated to finding the truth, and it gave me hope. I believed he would keep searching for answers and maybe find a way to fix this royal mess. Then someday in the distant future, I would receive his message as he had promised and this tragedy would have a happy ending. The weight of my guilt crushed me, and I could feel it eat away at my resolve. I wanted the hot water to melt it away, but not even a million scalding showers would be enough. How was I supposed to face my parents? How would was I supposed to act like I didn't know who they are? I don't know how long I spent sobbing and crying in the shower, but once I got out, my mind was made up. I needed to get myself out of this mess. But I had to be careful about it. I needed to give myself time to think through how I would do it.

I woke up the next day and my body felt just as stiff and sore as it had the day before. Convincing myself that I could make it through today, I dragged myself out of bed and washed my face, ignoring the massive dark circles that had formed under my eyes. Despite how depressed I felt, I put on a decent outfit, and that made me feel a little bit more human. Searching through my closet for the backpack I hadn't touched since the day I spoke to Anthony, I found the letter he had given me. I still didn't know what to do with it. I wasn't ready to give it directly to my stepmom and I wasn't ready to deal with all the questions she would fling at me.

Now that Anthony was dead, all this would do is cause more trouble than it was worth. The other option was to leave it somewhere she would conveniently stumble across it, but the chances of my father reaching it first were too high. Besides, I still did not know where Talika's allegiance lay. I decided to read the letter to see if the information in it would spark some wisdom on what to do next. Just as one would expect from Anthony, it was coded. At least that meant that if my father found it first, he wouldn't be able to read it. Still, it wasn't worth the risk, at least not at that moment. I put the letter back in the backpack and went on about my life like it didn't exist. I planned my escape from home for months, carefully biding my time and watching my parents like a hawk. Every move they made, every offhand comment, and every trip they took was cataloged in my mind. Figuring out how I would do it was hard, but once I had my plan, the games began. After I had completed the final phase of my plan, I snuck out of the house with my suitcase, making sure no one saw me, and hid it behind some bushes in the backyard.

I calmed my breathing, made my way to Molly's room, and hesitantly knocked on her door. I heard the familiar scrambling for a few seconds and then she opened the door.

"Yes dear, how can I help you?" she said with a genuine smile. It was refreshing to see someone that didn't seem to be burdened by any massive, life-ruining secrets, and I envied her. I shoved the little crumpled-up piece of paper into her hands. She looks up at me, almost offended by my actions. I would have been too if someone had casually handed me what looked like a piece of trash. Her face then melted into its default state, lips slightly curled in a diplomatic smile, and eyebrows lifted. I had learned a thing or two about hiding my emotions over the past few months and could see right through it.

"This is an important note for my mother. Do you remember the application I wanted to make?"

"Ahhh yes, I do my dear. I remember," she said, lowering her voice to a whisper. *"How did that go? Did you get what you needed?"*

"Yes, I did. Thank you so much for your help. I know it was a huge risk but I appreciate it."

"I am just glad I could help."

As she spoke she gave my shoulder a little squeeze. I could see the sincerity behind her words and felt a little guilty for dragging her into this mess.

"Please make sure that my father doesn't find out about this note. You know how he can be. But...," I looked directly into her eyes desperately waiting for her assurance and reassurance that she would keep my secret this one last time. She paused for what felt like ages but was probably no more than a few seconds and then nodded.

"My child, I don't know what is written in this letter, and by the look on your face, I think it's best if I don't know. But I see pain and sorrow in your eyes that cannot be denied. You may try to hide it, but that doesn't change the fact that it is there. So, you can count on me."

Her lips curled back into that familiar slight smile and I walked back knowing that this would probably be the last time I laid my eyes on her.

Once she was back inside, I quietly retrieved the suitcase from behind the bushes and left my home with no intention of ever coming back.

The Disadvantage Of Flight

I stood facing the woman I had spent my life believing was my mother, watching the tears stream from her eyes as I told her everything. Maria had returned at some point and sat silently on the edge of her bed with a look of disbelief plastered on her face. Talika hadn't tried to stop her, and I had failed to notice until that point. I threw all caution and care for consequences to the wind.

"That's why I had to leave, Talika."

These words cut through her like a hot blade and I could see it. But what was the point of pretending anymore? I wanted her to feel some of the pain I was feeling. Why did I have to bear this at all?

"So, you know everything, huh?" she scoffed.

"Yes, I do. I didn't want to believe that you were on their side but, by the looks of that pin on your collar, you are. How could you leave Anthony out to dry like that? Do you know how twisted that is?" I thought I would feel better now that I had let it all out, but I didn't. The knot in my gut was as tight as ever and my feet were cold and ached as the hard floor pulled all the heat from my body.

"I might not have birthed you Jaliya, but I raised you like my own. One man walks into

your life out of the blue and you are willing to throw 20 years out of the door like that. Yes, you are right; I lied to you and that is messed up. But I didn't create this situation. None of us wanted this."

"It's not about the fact that you didn't give birth to me. It's the fact that you continue to side with the people who killed both your sister, your father, and now your brother. I can't stomach how you can justify any of that!"

"Who exactly is the enemy in your story, Jaliya?"

This question caught me off-guard and I took a step back.

"What do you mean? The people that covered it up and anyone that chooses to side with them. How is this even a question?"

She looked at me and shook her head with a deep sigh.

"That brother of mine had to make one last mess for me to deal with before he died."

She walked over to the little couch in the corner and collapsed into it, throwing her head back and relaxing into the cushions and staring blankly at the roof. I honestly wanted to do the same, but my anger glued me to the floor. The blood had been boiling in my veins for so long that I think I had forgotten how to walk.

"So, you decided to blame me?"

"Of c...," I opened my mouth to speak, but she

cut me off.

"Just like Anthony, you needed someone to play the villain in your story, and I guess both times that just had to be me."

She began to cackle just like Anthony used to. It was as unsettling as his laugh, to say the least. They really were siblings.

"Do you have any idea how horrible of a person you are Jaliya?"

"ME?! Horrible?! After everything you let happen, you are calling **me** *a horrible person?"*

Her head shot up from its resting place and she looked me up and down.

"I have raised you like my own daughter for the past eighteen years and look how easily you've learned to resent me. You've spent the past couple of hours spewing nonsense about things you know nothing about with righteousness that rivals that of the gods. Guess what Jaliya; boohoo! Why don't you cry about it some more like the brat you are and have always been?"

My jaw dropped. Maria's jaw dropped as well. She knew better than to say anything, but we were both beyond speechless. I never expected such words from the woman I had known as my soft-spoken mother.

"Why do you look so shocked? You're not the only one that can say hurtful things,

*Jaliya. Here's a reality check, because you desperately need one. I lost my father, mother, sister, and now my brother. But I am the one you are taking all your anger on?! To save your ungrateful and frankly pitiful life, I was forced to marry your father. I gave up my education and my life to raise you, but **I'm** the villain?"*

"You stood by..."

"Shut up, Jaliya! Just shut up." She said,

finally sitting up.

"You're the hero, right? You're the good guy? You're the one that's going to stand up to Churchill and your father, right? The one that won't just stand by and let people keep getting hurt. You and Anthony both look down on me and call me weak. Well, take a good, long look in the mirror, child. At least I didn't run away. At least I am not in hiding. At least I made the sacrifices I had to make to protect the people I cared for and save what was left of my family. You don't

get to judge me, Jaliya. You are more of a coward than anyone of us."

Then Maria finally spoke, her quiet yet firm tone cutting through the highly emotional tone of the conversation.

"Listen, both of you, this is a difficult situation you have both put me in. You are both probably in grave danger right now, and this catfight needs to end."

She paused and buried her hand in her brow,

clearly fighting herself over something, and with
a deep sigh she said,
"I have to take both of you to Churchill before you
get yourselves killed."

To be continued........